"You seem desperate to keep your job."

Tallis's voice was even, cool. "I'm sure our director, Edgar Rankin, would view your employment with us in a much better light, Miss Underwood, if you ceased to be his son-in-law's mistress."

"Mistress!" Georgina flared. "How dare you!"

"Why bother to deny it?" Tallis York replied. "You and Desmond are seen everywhere together!"

"I hardly think being seen with Desmond makes me his mistress," Georgina insisted. "But despite your opinion, Mr. York, I will not stop seeing him." In the tense silence Georgina realized that she had overstepped the mark.

What was it about Tallis York that made Georgina, usually so composed, defy him? He was chairman of the company, and she was nothing more than an employee—perhaps now not even that!

The Other Woman

by

JESSICA STEELE

Harlequin Books

TORONTO • LONDON • LOS ANGELES • AMSTERDAM
SYDNEY • HAMBURG • PARIS • STOCKHOLM • ATHENS • TOKYO

Original hardcover edition published in 1980
by Mills & Boon Limited

ISBN 0-373-02370-7

Harlequin edition published November 1980

CHAPTER ONE

GEORGINA entered her office that Monday morning, but instead of going straight to her desk as she normally did, she paused at the door, glanced around the beige walls and surveyed the room. What would Mr Dixon, her new boss, make of it? she wondered, trying to see her office through his eyes. Not quite what he was used to, she couldn't help thinking. His office next door was a replica of hers, the same paint, dingy but unnoticed by her until today since she was so used to it. What would he make of the shabby desk and chair? She'd lost count of the times she had ruined her hose on the splintery legs of both her desk and the one next door, recalling that she had resorted to purchasing sandpaper and after removing strategically placed pieces of cellotape had rubbed away all of·the sharp but unseen hazards.

Chestertons (UK), now to be called 'Head Office', she supposed, lay on the other side of the city. Mr Dixon would find his new office very different from his old one, she felt sure. She had made a point of looking out for Chesterton House when it had become clear that Chestertons' bid for Parton and Naylor was being considered seriously. Chesterton House, she had taken particular note, was a modern building with the usual multitude of glass frontage interspersed with shiny masonry. She had stood gazing at it for some time, seeing the sturdiness of its structure and noting that it looked set to stand firm for years and years, unlike the building that housed the offices of Parton and Naylor, which looked ready to fall down at any given moment. She was willing to bet that no biting cold draught would dare to find its wintry way beneath the doors of Chesterton House. There would be no chance in that building of feet turning blue with cold as the staff sat at their desks.

Georgina came away from her office door and advanced into the room. She'd better get on. Mr Dixon would arrive soon, she thought, seeing it was his first day, but she had plenty to occupy herself with until he arrived.

She put her handbag away, musing that everything had moved fast once the Chesterton bid had been accepted. Her boss, Mr Parton, had retired on Friday, and today the new régime started. At first she had thought Chestertons were forcing Mr Parton to leave until he had told her he was looking forward to hanging up his slide rule and to spending more time with his ailing wife. Then as his talk of retirement had sunk in, Georgina had experienced disquiet about her own position within the company. For all their run-down appearance, Parton and Naylor paid better than most, and her salary was essential to not only her, but to Maggie and the children. She just couldn't afford to take months and months looking for a job that equalled this one in salary. That cheque must be sent home to Maggie each month. Whether the panic she had felt had not been so well concealed as she had thought, she didn't know, but her relief was boundless when Mr Parton told her:

'Chestertons are sending in one of their people to take my place. I've met Vincent Dixon, I'm sure you'll like him.'

At ten o'clock that Monday morning Georgina looked at her watch. No Mr Dixon yet. Perhaps they kept different hours at Chestertons, she thought whimsically, then buried her head in her work again. At ten-thirty, her mind completely absorbed, she stretched out a hand absently to answer the phone when it rang.

'Mr Parton's secretary,' she said with the custom of usage, only to bring her mind back from the matter she was checking to realise she was no longer Mr Parton's secretary.

'Miss Underwood?' the female voice queried before she could correct her statement.

'Yes,' Georgina agreed, not recognising the voice.

'Oh, good morning. This is Chestertons (UK).' Georgina's face quirked silently. Mr Dixon had called in at Head Office before coming here, she decided, expecting to be asked to hold on while they connected her through to him. It was thoughtful of him to call to say he'd been delayed. 'Could you manage to be here at twelve-thirty?' the efficient-sounding voice went on.

'You want me to come there?' Georgina asked, barely able to hide her surprise.

'Twelve-thirty if that's convenient,' said the voice.

'Well—yes,' said Georgina, wondering what the voice would come back with if she said she couldn't make it. 'What...' she began, about to ask the perfectly reasonable question, she thought, of why she should be asked to call at Chestertons.

'Ask for Mrs Fry at reception,' she was instructed before she could put the question. 'Goodbye, Miss Underwood.'

Her mind now completely off the work she had been doing, Georgina replaced the telephone and stared at it with unseeing eyes. Why the dickens had she to cross the city and present herself at Chestertons (UK)? And who was Mrs Fry? And where was Mr Dixon?

Suddenly the fear that had beset her when Mr Parton had told her he was retiring again had her in its grip.

Wasn't Mr Dixon coming in to take his place after all? Was she, despite what had been said about the takeover not affecting the position of any of the staff, about to be made redundant after all? Oh no, they wouldn't do that would they? Mr Parton had said there would be no redundancies. She tried to gain some comfort from that thought, but she couldn't find any. Mr Parton no longer had anything to do with the company. Chestertons could go back on their word and there wasn't a thing he could do about it.

Georgina tried to immerse herself in her work until such time as she need leave for her twelve-thirty appointment, but it was useless. Trying to keep calm, telling herself she was foolish to imagine the worst, she went to the cabinet that housed the Chesterton file looking through every piece of correspondence for the name Fry. It didn't appear anywhere—she even checked their headed paper. No one by the name of Mrs Fry was a director or manager; she hadn't really expected her to be, no one of such standing would have time to waste with anyone so far down the business scale as a lowly secretary of the Parton and Naylor outfit. Senior secretary, she reminded herself, pride coming to her aid as the suspicion grew that this Mrs Fry was Chestertons' personnel manager, and that at twelve-thirty she would be hearing something she would very much rather not hear.

Checking her watch once more, Georgina picked up her bag and went to the cloakroom. There she washed her hands, ran a comb through honey-blonde hair that grew straight until it reached just below her nape and then curled loosely under. She straightened up, having had to bend her five feet six inches to peer into the low-hung mirror. Then backing away from the mirror to get a full

view of herself in her grey suit and pink shirt, her beauti-
fully shaped mouth unsmiling, she surveyed her image. No
one at Chestertons was going to have an inkling of the
dread she was feeling. She would be twenty-six this month,
had been in London for just over six years, and over that
time had hidden her warm nature from all but her family
and perhaps Mr Parton and Desmond. The picture that
now looked back at her had the sophistication she had
aimed at, had the coolness that had killed the ardour of
more than one member of the opposite sex who had thought
to get to know her better. She wasn't interested in affairs
and it would be years yet before she could consider marriage.

A determined look crossed her face as she made her way
from the cloakroom. If she was going to have to say goodbye to her job, then this Mrs Fry, if she was the one who
had been selected to do the deed, was going to hear from
her what she thought of Chestertons' methods in leading
Mr Parton up the garden path with all that guff about Mr
Dixon coming to take his place.

Georgina left the building. She had thought she should
tell someone where she was going, but who was there to
tell? Mr Naylor would be deep in dictation with his
secretary, and even if she did tell him about her sus-
picions of this interview he wouldn't be able to do anything. She was used to handling her own crises anyway,
though she felt the weight of responsibility that this
particular crisis was one that didn't affect only her. If
she had to take a job that paid less than this one, the
repercussions of that would rebound heavily on Maggie,
Josh and Nicola.

Only anyone with acute discernment who looked into
the deeply blue eyes of the sophisticated-looking young

lady who walked away from the offices of Parton and Naylor would see that she was nowhere near as confident as she appeared.

Once through the swish door of Chesterton House, Georgina, her chin tilted a fraction higher than normal, crossed the thickly carpeted foyer and went straight to the reception desk.

'I'm Georgina Underwood,' she told the smart-looking young woman on duty. 'I have an appointment with Mrs Fry.'

'Twelve-thirty, wasn't it?' she answered pleasantly. 'You're a few minutes early, but if you'd like to take the elevator to the top of the building you'll find Mrs Fry's office, the third door on the left.'

Georgina thanked her and wheeled in the direction of the elevators. Her stomach began to churn over as the elevator ascended. She knew she couldn't put it down to the movement of the elevator, there seeming to be no sensation of moving at all. She stepped out of the elevator on the top floor, saw no one about and took a few calming breaths before making for the door the receptionist had directed. Her firm knock on the door was answered immediately by, 'Come in.'

Georgina went in, and wasn't fooled for an instant by the smile on the woman's face who looked up from her typewriter, not until the woman said, 'Miss Underwood? Good. He won't be too long. If you'd like to take a seat for a moment,' and then Georgina realised that Mrs Fry wasn't the person she had been asked here to see, but *he*, whoever *he* was, and that Mrs Fry's smile was perfectly genuine.

She took the seat Mrs Fry had indicated, deciding Mrs Fry must be *his* secretary. Was *he* the personnel manager, then?

'Would you mind if I carried on with my typing, I don't seem to be getting on very well today?'

Georgina looked at the woman, calculated she was somewhere in her middle thirties and looked a shade under the weather. Perhaps she's got a cold coming, she thought, as she replied, 'No, of course not,' before turning her eyes to take in the room. Maybe it was because she was so used to the shabby interior of her own office back at Parton's, but the office Mrs Fry worked in could only be described as plush. A delicate shade of green adorned the walls, carpet on the floor was a darker shade of green, and she'd like to bet Mrs Fry had never once pulled her hose on that most modern of desks. The electric typewriter Mrs Fry was using seemed to be the most up to date, and although she was transcribing from shorthand, Georgina noted that there was the latest in dictaphone machines near at hand.

Then all interest in the office and its equipment faded, for the intercom buzzed and she just knew she was about to be summoned through the only other door in the room apart from the one she had come in by. Mrs Fry flicked a switch and Georgina's stomach began a renewed churning over. And then the churning stopped, because suddenly pride mingled with an unexpected rush of temper. For the voice that came through the intercom, crisp, and oh, so confident, said:

'Send Miss Underwood in, please, Mrs Fry.'

She didn't like his confidence even before she saw him. It annoyed her that he was so sure the little secretary from Parton and Naylor would drop everything to rush to obey his summons, he hadn't even bothered to ask, 'Has Miss Underwood arrived?' and certainly Mrs Fry hadn't buzzed through to say she was here. He had just taken it for granted she was there. She stood up, her chin at a haughty angle.

'Mr York will see you now,' said Mrs Fry, turning to her.

'Mr York?' Georgina questioned, her temper leaving as she fought to hide her astonishment. 'Mr Tallis York?'

'That's right,' smiled Mrs Fry. 'It wouldn't do to keep him waiting.'

Georgina veiled her eyes, her thoughts chaotic as she turned towards the door she was to go through. Tallis York wanted to see *her*! Without reading the headed paper of Chestertons' this morning that told her Tallis York was the chairman of the whole shoot, she clearly remembered his signature, his writing bold and no-nonsense about it, as indeed his letter had been straight and to the point. And he wanted to see her!

She paused, her fingers on the handle of his door, no time now to get any of the thoughts that were tumbling in into any sort of order. In a very few seconds she would be facing the chairman of Chestertons (UK), Chestertons (Overseas), and lord knew how many subsidiary companies. Her head held high, Georgina turned the handle and went in.

At once she observed that the man who was looking her way was a man who never wasted a spare moment. Apparently she had taken a minute too long in answering his, 'Send Miss Underwood in', for he was now engaged in a telephone conversation. She turned to close the door, then facing the room again saw that his eyes were still on her, saw his eyes flick over her figure before returning to her face, and while his authoritative voice gave orders down the phone, his flow remained uninterrupted as he completed his inspection of her. Some of her hauteur returned as she looked back at him. She guessed he would be tall when he stood up, saw he had night-black hair and eyes that appeared night-black to match. He had a tough, hard-hitting look to him, his mouth firm and giving an impression of cruelty till one studied his bottom lip.

For no reason the word 'lover' shot into her head and she looked away from him for the first time. She knew why that word had separated itself from all the others, she thought. There was a hint of sensuality in that bottom lip that told her he had not reached his age—what was it, thirty-seven, thirty-eight?—without having his share of paramours. She brought her mind hastily away from such thoughts—what was she doing thinking about such things anyway?—She was sure she wasn't remotely interested in his love life. It was just that in some odd way this man's presence seemed to arouse in her a sexual awareness she had never before been so instantly conscious of.

Her eyes lit on the matching dictaphone set he had in his office, a brother to the one she had seen in Mrs Fry's office, then she forgot about it entirely as she revised her ideas on why she had been summoned. It couldn't be that she was going to be made redundant after all, she thought, some of her wilting confidence returning. By no stretch of the imagination would the lordly chairman of Chestertons be the one to tell her her services were no longer required. Perhaps he wanted to know something he had forgotten to ask Mr Parton—though she couldn't see this man forgetting anything; perhaps he thought she could tell him the answer without him having to bother Mr Parton in his retirement. She had dealt with many confidential matters, after all. Though why she had to present herself here when she could see he was more than capable of lifting up a telephone... Her thoughts came to an abrupt end as he finished his call.

He leaned back in his chair looking relaxed and casual,

but there was a shrewdness in his eyes, she thought, that only the most unwary would be foolish to disregard. He stretched out one capable-looking hand indicating the chair nearest to the side of his desk, and she caught a glimpse of platinum cuff links securing the cuffs of his blue shirt that showed beneath the dark material of his suit jacket.

'Take a seat, Miss Underwood,' he drawled.

Georgina was conscious of his eyes following her every movement as she came further into the room and sat down. He wasn't interested in the usual courtesies, then, she thought, swallowing down the 'good morning' she had ready, though since it was after twelve, 'good afternoon' would have been more correct.

'You wanted to see me, I believe,' she said, feeling a shade uncomfortable when he didn't add anything to his instruction that she be seated. Her words had come out coolly, and she was glad about that. She rather thought they matched her sophisticated image, but she saw, infinitesimal though it had been, a flicker of something in his eyes as her tone registered, then it was gone.

'So you're Georgina Underwood,' he said, then agreed softly, 'Oh yes, Miss Underwood, I wanted to see you.'

For all his words were quietly spoken, she sensed there was an ominous touch of aggression lying in wait there somewhere. She tried to think of anything she had done wrong while working for Mr Parton that could in any way have unfortunate repercussions for the new owners, but could think of nothing. Give or take the occasional hiccup or two, everything back at Parton and Naylor was running as smoothly as ever.

'You said that as though you believe I'm in error in some way,' she said, taking the battle straight into his camp since he seemed in no hurry to enlighten her as to what she was doing here. Though why she should think of it as a battle she didn't know. Maybe it was because she was aware of a mighty aggression lurking somewhere in the man sitting across from her, oh, so coolly watching her every reaction.

'Far be it for me to judge the error of your ways,' he said, turning what she had said around and not making it sound very pleasant, before going smoothly on. 'But when your name is brought as constantly to my notice as it has been these past weeks, and when this morning I have the problem of Georgina Underwood thrust before me yet again, I thought it high time I had a look at you.'

Only just did Georgina save her eyes from going wide and thereby revealing her surprise. It came as a shock to her that the chairman of Chestertons so much as knew her name, much less to hear that he thought she was a problem. And what exactly did he mean by the 'error of her ways'? Unconsciously she straightened in her chair, a matching glint of aggression showing itself.

'I can't think why I should be so much discussed, Mr York,' she said, hanging on tightly to her composure.

Tallis York ignored her comment as though she had never made it. Then his eyes did a slow and thorough tour of her, though she was sure he had missed nothing of her in his first inspection. Then, deliberately she thought, he said :

'I can't say that I can fault Warner's taste.'

'Warner?' Georgina queried. She hadn't liked Tallis York's insolent appraisal of her, liked even less that the conversation looked to be moving into personal channels— she was here on business—and she didn't think either that he had meant to be complimentary when he had said he couldn't fault Warner's taste. Who the heck was Warner? The only Warner she knew was Desmond, but surely...

'Desmond . . .' she began hesitatingly, only to see that any pretence of being agreeable had left Tallis York as the hardness she had suspected in the man came through.

'Desmond Warner,' he confirmed, nothing easy in his manner now, as he went back to the problem of Georgina Underwood, giving her the impression that even though he appeared to know Desmond, his name had been mentioned as an incidental. 'Ever since the takeover of Parton and Naylor was first muted,' he told her, 'it has been cluttered up with a side issue of one Georgina Underwood.'

'Cluttered . . .' Georgina tried, in a complete fog as to what she, who had never heard of any of the high-ups at Chestertons, much less met any of them, should as secretary to Mr Parton be capable of cluttering up anything to do with the negotiations. She wasn't allowed to add anything to that one word 'Cluttered'.

'It was important if the deal was to go through without any time-consuming hold-ups for agreement to be reached with regard to there being no terminations of employment,' he told her. 'Both Mr Parton and Mr Naylor were adamant about that. I myself was perfectly agreeable to it too—as I see it we shall need to take on more staff, not lay people off.' Georgina tried to stay with him, but as quick-thinking as she normally was, she was having difficulty in working out why he was telling her all this.

She got as far as asking, 'But what has all this to do with me?' before she was favoured with a frowning glance as though Tallis York thought she already knew, and was playing some devious game of her own. She could tell that he didn't care much for her interruption.

'I'll tell you what it has to do with you,' he said coldly. 'Thanks to your—friendship—with Warner, the whole negotiations almost came to grief.'

'My friendship with Desmond!' Georgina gasped, realising Desmond's name hadn't come up incidentally after all, but wondering if the chairman of Chestertons had suddenly had a brain storm. How could her friendship with Desmond wreck the takeover? She wanted to laugh, it was so ridiculous. The desire to laugh vanished rapidly as she looked at Tallis York; there was no spark of humour to be seen in those dark eyes as he informed her:

'Edgar Rankin was coming down hard in his insistence that there should be at least one redundancy.'

Her mind caught at the name Edgar Rankin and while Tallis York waited for the name to sink in, she recalled from the Chesterton headed paper she had taken special note of that morning that Edgar Rankin was a director of the company. It therefore followed that he was on the board. Was he a dissenting voice to the takeover? Had his opposition to be overcome? But she had never met this Edgar Rankin, and Desmond didn't know him either she was sure. He had never mentioned him anyway. And then Edgar Rankin and Desmond both took a back seat as what Tallis York had said about Edgar Rankin wanting at least one redundancy took hold. There was one person he wanted out before he would cast his vote for the takeover to be proceeded with, she thought with fast growing alarm. Was it her? It must be. Yet she couldn't begin to think that there might have been a row, probably at board room level over her. She couldn't even begin to know what this Edgar Rankin had got against her.

The terrible anxiety grew within her that her security was being threatened and with it grew the conviction that the person Edgar Rankin wanted to get rid of was her. And as her feeling of insecurity ballooned out of proportion, her fear of what it would mean to Maggie and the children if she lost her well paying job, unnerved Georgina too much to worry about Edgar Rankin and what all this had to do with Desmond; all she knew was she had to have the answer to the one question that surmounted all others.

'You've called me here to tell me I'm to be dismissed,' she said, looking across at the man seated nearby, her voice coming from a suddenly parched throat. She saw Tallis York giving her a considering look as the hoarse words left her.

'Your job obviously means a lot to you,' he observed, then informed her, as she had previously worked out for herself that the chairman of a vast concern such as Chestertons would have other people to do that sort of job for him. 'It's many years since I personally dismissed anyone.' The way he said it left her in no doubt that he still had the stomach to do his own dirty work if he found it necessary.

'This Mr Rankin wants me out, though, doesn't he?' she questioned, feeling none the better for knowing Tallis York wasn't going to be the one to tell her to look for alternate employment.

He didn't answer her question, and she had a clear impression that he thought she knew more than she was letting on. Had a clear impression Tallis York thought she knew all about Edgar Rankin and that she was just playing dumb for her own ends.

'Aside from the fact I thought it about time I had a look at the particular thorn in Edgar's side, there is another reason I wanted to see you,' Tallis York went on.

Georgina's mind set off searching in all directions. She was growing a mite calmer now, her confidence still not what she would like it to be, but her throat was feeling less dry as she tried for a cool voice that would give away nothing of the torment of her mind.

'Mr Dixon?' she plucked out of nowhere, about to add

she didn't think much of any company who could lead a retiring head of another company on to believe someone was coming in to take his place. She was glad she paused before she spoke her thoughts out loud, because Tallis York was agreeing:

'Yes, Vincent Dixon. Unfortunately he was involved in a car accident over the weekend. From what his doctors tell me, it will be all of three months before he'll be fit enough to give you any dictation.'

Several points isolated themselves at once from what she had just been told, one of them being that it wasn't any myth that this Vincent Dixon was coming in to take over from Mr Parton. Another thing that penetrated was that Tallis York had somehow found the time to have a personal word with Mr Dixon's doctors. And a very big and important third fact emerged; the most important fact of all in the labyrinth of all her thoughts was that despite Edgar Rankin's opposition it looked as though Tallis York intended to keep his word to Mr Parton about there being no redundancies, because he had spoken of Vincent Dixon giving *her* dictation when he returned.

'Are you saying . . .' she began, her voice sounding husky so that sophisticated image or not she just had to break off to clear it as the suspense got the better of her. She swallowed, then tried again, glad to hear her voice sounding more normal. 'Are you saying that when Mr Dixon does take up his post at Parton and Naylor I'm to be his secretary?'

'If that's what you wish,' Tallis York told her coolly, his keen eyes sharp on her face, causing her to hope she was less pale than she felt. 'Mr Parton tells me you're the most efficient secretary he had ever had, I have no reason to disbelieve him. I'm sure you and Vincent Dixon will work well together.'

'But,' said Georgina, awash with relief and wishing she had the sense to keep her mouth closed now that her anxieties for the future seemed to be over, 'does this Mr Rankin still want me dismissed?'

She saw Tallis York's left eyebrow ascend at her again, saying, '*This* Mr Rankin'. Evidently he wasn't believing she hadn't a clue why Edgar Rankin should have taken such great exception to her.

'It's beside the point whether he does or not,' she was told coldly. 'I'm not likely to want the whole of the workforce at Parton and Naylor wondering about the security of their own jobs should I bow to pressure and get rid of someone on the secretarial staff when the efficiency of her work had never been questioned.'

Georgina wished she knew when to leave well enough alone. But from that statement Tallis York had just made it was obvious to her he had resisted all Edgar Rankin's attempts to get her out but that the pressure was still being applied. And she knew it would niggle away at her when she got back to her own office if she hadn't made any attempt to learn what this Edgar Rankin had against her.

'Why does Edgar Rankin want me dismissed?' she asked, and received Tallis York's long level look for her pains. She knew then he would only tell her if he felt like doing so, but she didn't have to wait very long to discover that he couldn't see any reason why she shouldn't be informed.

'Because he happens to be a particularly doting father,' he told her obscurely.

The news that Edgar Rankin was a doting father was no enlightenment to Georgina at all. Many fathers doted on their offspring. She couldn't see that that was any reason for this particular father to want to get her out of the organisation.

'Edgar Rankin just happens to worship the ground his daughter walks on,' Tallis York added when Georgina just sat there with every appearance of being mystified. He then began to look as though he had had enough of what he thought was her play-acting and brought her friend Desmond's name into the conversation again by saying bluntly, 'You know of course that Warner is a married man?'

The switch from their conversation of Edgar Rankin and his adored daughter had Georgina's confusion growing. She wondered briefly if Tallis York had deliberately tossed Desmond's name at her to unseat her returning confidence. For it didn't take two guesses to see that had she not known Desmond was married then Tallis York was making no apology that he was the one to inform her of that fact.

'Lara—Desmond's wife—walked out on him twelve months ago,' she said shortly, feeling annoyed as much with herself as Tallis York that she was sounding as though she was trying to exonerate herself for being friends with Desmond by explaining that he and his wife were separated.

'You know Lara?' he asked sharply.

'We have met,' said Georgina edgily, gathering that he too knew Lara, but not liking his sharp tone.

She didn't like this whole conversation either, she thought, her annoyance getting the better of her that he seemed to think he could take the conversation down any avenue he chose regardless of whether it mattered to her or not. She didn't care then if she never knew why Edgar Rankin objected so strongly to her working for Chestertons. Tallis York had told her her job was secure and she could understand his not wanting the other workers to feel their jobs threatened. In a period where first-class craftsmen were hard to come by he wouldn't want to risk unrest in the works and for some of the highly skilled men to walk out on him. She took a deep breath in an endeavour to control the anger that had risen up in her.

'If it's all the same to you, Mr York,' she said with hard fought for control, 'I would prefer my personal life to be kept personal. It has no bearing whatsoever on the way in which I carry out my duties, and I just cannot see any possible reason why you should bring my friendship with Desmond Warner into a business discussion.'

For a long moment there was silence in the streamlined office. She saw his eyes narrow as she delivered her little speech. He had a ruthless look about him, and she had a feeling none of his employees had ever dared to speak to him the way in which she had just done. Then while his dark eyes continued to hold hers, she saw the hard look of him relax, and while that shrewdness was forever in his eyes, his voice was quiet when next he spoke.

'You're desperate to keep your job, aren't you?' he observed coolly, telling her if she didn't already know it that it hadn't gone unnoticed by him that he had shaken her out of her sophisticated pose when she had thought her job was going to be taken away from her. Then, his manner remaining cool, he left her in no doubt as to the hardness in him. 'I think we had better get one thing straight right away, Miss Underwood,' he told her, no pretence at being agreeable about him now. 'While you're sitting in that chair, for however long I continue to pay you, we shall discuss whatever I decide is appropriate to be discussed.'

Never had Georgina been spoken to in such a commanding way. She couldn't have said anything then even if her brain had been able to come up with anything cogent to insert. Tallis York hadn't raised his voice, but there was unbendable steel there and she knew it.

'If I decide in the interests of this company that there are certain matters of your private life that need to be gone into, then regardless of any timid feelings you might have on the niceness of that discussion, make no mistake, I shall do so.'

For all he managed to look relaxed, there was no arguing against that tone, and much though it went against the grain to sit there quietly and take it, at that moment she just didn't trust him not to rescind his statement that the job of Vincent Dixon's secretary was hers if she so wished.

Hating herself for not being in a position where she could tell him exactly what he could do with his job, and likewise anything of a personal nature he had to say to her, Georgina swallowed down her ire.

'Very well, Mr York,' she said, stamping hard on the impulse to throw caution to the winds and tell him what he could do with the job anyway. 'You've made it obvious that I have no choice but to sit here and listen to what you have to say,' and if he didn't gather from that that she thought anything he had to say was just not worth listening to, then she had misread her man.

But if she had thought she could bandy words with him and come out the victor she soon found herself very much mistaken. His voice was almost silky as he relaxed back into his chair again, rubbed a considering hand across his chin and said:

'Just in case you aren't aware of the fact, Edgar Rankin happens to be Lara Warner's father.'

'Lara's father!' Georgina exclaimed, some of her poise deserting her as Tallis York dropped out that startling piece of news. On the very rare occasions that Desmond had ever mentioned his father-in-law, it had only ever been as 'Lara's father', never at any time could she remember Desmond referring to him as Mr Rankin.

And then, before she could think further about this

latest piece of startling news, before she could begin to tie it all up with what it all had to do with Edgar Rankin wanting her employment terminated, Tallis York was laying it on the line so that she couldn't possibly mistake what the purpose of her visit to Head Office was all about.

'I've already told you how Edgar Rankin dotes on his daughter,' he reminded her. 'It's precisely because of his devotion to her, his desire to ensure that Lara never knows a moment's anguish, never knows a moment's hurt—hurt, I may say, that he believes you, through Warner, have inflicted on her,' he ignored that Georgina's eyes grew wide at that last statement and continued, 'that he has been at pains to have you removed from the payroll. Ever since the takeover of Parton and Naylor got under way and he became aware that you were in their employ, I've had him breathing down my neck to agree to your dismissal.'

'But ...' Georgina tried to interrupt, only to find she was wasting her breath. Tallis York had come to the crunch of the matter. If he had been soft-pedalling with her before that had ceased five minutes ago when she had challenged him that she didn't want to discuss her private life.

He looked straight into her deep blue eyes and told her without a glimmer of emotion showing, 'Not to put too fine a point on it, I object strongly to being petitioned at every opportunity to get rid of you. But for other reasons I find myself in a position of having to put up with it.'

Georgina wondered what those other reasons were. She wouldn't have thought a man in his position would have to put up with anything that didn't suit him, though she conceded he was probably referring to the harmony of the boardroom. No doubt there were many differences of opinion at that level, but as chairman it was his responsibility to keep things running as smoothly as possible. But what was he saying about ...

'As I mentioned before,' Tallis York's voice cut across her thoughts, 'your name came up again this morning. It was in relation to Vincent Dixon's accident and you being without a direct boss. I thought then it was about time I had a look at the female who's growing to be as big an irritant to me as she is to Edgar Rankin.' And then his jaw, she had thought, showed a certain ruthlessness, really proved itself, for leaning forward, he told her in no uncertain terms, 'I'm very much afraid, Miss Underwood, that if we're both to get our hearts' desire—you keep the job that means so much to you, and I to get some peace from Edgar—then you really will have to do something about Warner.'

'Warner?' Georgina gasped.

'I think, Miss Underwood, you will have to give serious consideration to withdrawing your favours from Warner.' And while she just sat there not fully comprehending his meaning, he enlightened her so fully that she was almost gasping with outrage. 'I'm certain,' he said easily, 'that Edgar Rankin will view your employment with us in a much better light if you ceased being Warner's mistress.'

CHAPTER TWO

'*Mistress!*' So great was the shock of hearing herself being called Desmond Warner's mistress that Georgina was on her feet without knowing she had risen. 'How dare you!' she flared, only to find Tallis York ignoring her fury.

'Why bother to deny it?' he asked coolly, in no way affected that she looked furious enough to blow a fuse as he pushed his chair away from his desk and got casually to his feet. As she had expected he was tall, and towered over her as he looked down at her with a sardonic look. 'It's common knowledge that you and Warner are seen everywhere together.'

'Being seen about with Desmond doesn't make me his mistress,' Georgina said hotly, and would have said more only it seemed that Tallis York wasn't interested in any defence she had to put forward.

'You said yourself Lara left him twelve months ago,' he reminded her, folding his arms and leaning to rest the backs of his thighs against his desk, this action serving to bring to her attention the fact that his aplomb was in no way disturbed that she was raging angry. 'Warner is no woman-shy male,' he told her. 'He was married to Lara for almost a year before she left him. He's used to having a woman in his bed. You don't seriously expect me to believe that since you're the only woman with whom his name has been linked, your relationship with him is that of merely just "good friends".'

Georgina was fairly spluttering with outrage. 'Yes, I do,' she said heatedly, and could see by the way his mouth curled up derisively at one corner that he didn't think much of anyone who had to hide behind what he thought were lies. 'Desmond and I are friends and no more than that,' she added, none of her heat leaving her.

'You're trying to tell me Warner has spent these last twelve months in complete celibacy?' he derided. 'Come off it, Miss Underwood. From your file I see you're almost twenty-six, you yourself must have been playing in the grown-ups' league for some years now. I can't see that either of you have been dating each other for twelve months and are still at the hand-holding stage.' About to insert that she had been going out with Desmond for nine months, not twelve, she found the moment was lost when

Tallis York scoffed, 'Are you trying to tell me that Warner has never so much as kissed those inviting lips of yours?'

'Yes—No—I...' Georgina began, his reference to her inviting lips throwing her. Desmond had kissed her last New Year's Eve, but it had only been a chaste kiss. She delayed too long in saying so and received a further derisory look that said he had read in her hesitation that Desmond had kissed her, and that he rested his case.

'It's not what you think,' she tried, but could see he wasn't going to believe her.

'Of course it isn't,' Tallis York mocked, his mockery infuriating her further, making her forget that to him she must appear to be the nonentity of a secretary from across the city.

'Don't judge Desmond by your own standards!' she flared, coming off the defence for the first time since his accusation, as her temper went wildly out of control.

In the tense silence that followed her words, Georgina knew she had overstepped the mark as the mocking air fell away from the chairman of Chestertons.

'Would you care to explain that statement?' he asked with menacing quiet.

Her temper left her. Oh dear, he looked ready to throw her out of his office for her insolence! Then anger spurted again and came to her aid. Just who did he think he was that he could hurl insults at her and not be paid back in kind?

'I think it highly unlikely that there has been a twelve-month celibacy period in your life since you—er—entered the "grown-up league",' she said, refusing to back down. He had virility written all over him. She was sure her accusation was well founded.

Unbelievably, she saw her attack had amused him; the hard look had gone from him anyway. She saw the corner of his mouth move before his humour was repressed. Then he lifted up his wrist to note the time by his watch and she realised he had probably given her far more time than he allowed any one of his staff.

'Your thoughts on my celibacy, or lack of it, sound most interesting, Miss Underwood. Unfortunately I have no time to allow you to expand on that theme.' The eyes that had been glinting threateningly at her only a short time before now had a definite hint of devilment in them, she thought. 'Trot back to your office now, I'll be in touch with you again.'

Ready to depart, though not liking that 'Trot back to your office' which well and truly relegated her into the lower echelons, though it could have been just a figure of speech, she supposed, Georgina was arrested by his, 'I'll be in touch with you again.' What did that mean? That his discussion about her relationship with Desmond wasn't finished? That for the sake of peace and quiet, he would try to get her to give Desmond up?

'I shan't stop seeing Desmond,' she told him spiritedly.

'I hardly expected that you would,' he replied, 'though I thought the idea worth mentioning. I can see now I was right in my first surmise. Things have gone too far between the two of you.'

Casually he strolled to the door with her and opened it for her to go through. And Georgina bit down on the retort she could have made that things between her and Desmond had gone precisely nowhere. It would take a battering ram to get it through Tallis York's obstinate skull.

'Goodbye, Mr York,' she said firmly, crossing the threshold into the outer office.

'Goodbye, Miss Underwood,' Tallis York replied with a return of his mocking air, and closed the door on her.

Georgina noted that Mrs Fry wasn't at her desk, but she didn't need to look at her watch to know her interview with Tallis York had gone on well into the lunch hour.

She was too annoyed and confused to want to bother with lunch herself, her mind going over every part of her conversation with Tallis York as she made her way back to Parton and Naylor.

It was difficult to decide which part of what had occurred at Chesterton House to dissect first. That Edgar Rankin had his knives out and sharpened for her was obvious. Equally obvious was the fact that Lara must have been laying it on thick about her friendship with Desmond. But why should she? The remedy was in Lara's own hands. It was she who had left Desmond, not the other way about, and she must know that Desmond wanted her back. Georgina thought for a while about what Desmond had told her about his marriage break-up, of how the early days of the marriage had been pretty tempestuous.

'I didn't worry about the rows over-much,' she recalled him telling her. 'Both Lara and I are used to having our own way, but I thought the love we had for each other was enough to get us over that first troubled year—it's common knowledge that every marriage has a few teething troubles in the early days.' Georgina remembered vividly the heart-breaking sadness in his face that his marriage had barely survived that first year as he had gone on to tell her about the blazing row that had culminated in Lara leaving him. 'We were just getting over one stormy patch and then Lara's father had the grand idea of me joining his firm.' Georgina saw now that the firm was Chestertons. 'The old boy told Lara that everything augured well for me having a seat on the board in next to no time.'

Desmond hadn't needed to tell her that the idea of him being on the board would have infinite appeal to Lara. She had observed for herself that the girl from a well-to-do background was a grade A snob when they had bumped into her and her escort at the theatre during one of the intervals. She had fast been forming that opinion of her, and it was cemented when she caught the whispered taunt Lara made to him that she knew she wasn't supposed to have heard. 'Still toiling night and day trying to make something out of that tatty factory, Desmond?' she had jibed. Georgina had turned her head away to make some polite remark to Lara's escort, but not before she had seen the tight look that had come over Desmond's face.

That Desmond had remained adamant in his refusal to give up his small engineering works, enjoying the work he did, even if it was barely off the ground yet, was the root cause for Lara deciding to pack her bags and return to her father, Desmond had told her. Though she privately thought the teething troubles he had spoken of must have added to Lara's decision to leave him. To be fair to Desmond he never actually ran Lara down, but as he saw it, his marriage would be worth nothing if he gave in on this point.

Georgina left thinking about Tallis York until last, hoping that by the time she let herself dwell on anything he had said her blood would have cooled to below boiling point. But remembering his dark sadonic look, that look said he wasn't going to believe she and Desmond weren't lovers no matter how much she protested, she knew if she put off thinking about him until the moon grew pink spots she would still feel the same outrage that he had *dared* to make his vile accusation.

It went without saying that he had been around, and then some. And to be fair, though she damned her innate honesty that afforded him that concession, then she supposed there were masses of girls in this day and age who were rising twenty-six who had had the experience he was laying at her door. But to actually accuse her of it!

She went home that night knowing that to go over her interview with Tallis York yet again would be fruitless. Her mind had spun with thinking about it during the afternoon, so that she had deliberately had to turn her mind to how she was going to cope without Vincent Dixon in Mr Parton's chair. Fortunately, as the circumstances now turned out, Mr Parton had always been far more interested in machinery than in office work, so she didn't anticipate too many problems, since he was more often than not to be found in the works than his office, and she was used to handling things on her own.

Letting herself into her apartment, she found she just didn't have any appetite for food. She blamed Tallis and his nasty mind for that, and decided she would do a few routine jobs first and maybe eat later.

She concentrated her thoughts on Desmond as she pattered about her small flat. Should she tell him what had gone on today or not? Not, she decided, after much thought. He had been dashing about from here to Belgium for six weeks, the last three of which she hadn't seen him at all. He was due back home today, hopefully with his order book full, for that had been the purpose of his constant to-ing and fro-ings. Oh, she so hoped he had got what he had been after. If he had, how could she dim his excitement by telling him? Sometimes he was very down, and if he hadn't succeeded in Belgium, then how could she flatten him further by telling him that Edgar Rankin was trying to lose her her job, and the interpretation Tallis York had put on their friendship? Then she remembered, that of course Desmond didn't know about the takeover yet. She realised then that if she hadn't still regarded the matter as confidential she would have told

Desmond about it the last time she had seen him. He would then, she was sure, have told her of his father-in-law's connection with Chestertons.

He couldn't have seen Lara either recently, she reasoned, or Lara would have told him that Chestertons had put in a bid for Parton and Naylor and he would have mentioned it. She knew Lara occasionally agreed to dine with him, and had thought that meant Lara still loved him, but their meetings never ended amicably, and he was never the best of company for days afterwards. Instinct told her that if Desmond had pulled off his deal, then he would be bound to ring Lara as soon as he was back in England. He would be eager to tell someone of his success—who better than the woman he loved?

When the phone rang just before eight Georgina was in the middle of deciding what most of the things she had in her food cupboard did she fancy for her meal. She came out of her tiny kitchen and into her sitting room-cum-dining room, and picked up the phone.

'Desmond!' she exclaimed delightedly on hearing his voice. 'I didn't expect to hear from you tonight.'

'I got back today,' said Desmond, as though suspecting she had forgotten.

'Yes, I know, but I thought...' She broke off, realising it wouldn't be very tactful to say she thought he would be out dining with Lara, especially if the reason he wasn't celebrating with his wife was because his negotiations in Belgium had proved fruitless. 'Er—how's business?' she asked tentatively, ready with her sympathy, even an invitation round to share her supper if he was in low spirits.

A share of her supper wasn't needed, though she was unsure about the sympathy as he told her, 'Business is fine. I landed the Belgium contract.'

'Oh, Desmond, that's marvellous!' said Georgina, truly

delighted for him. Then, her voice faltering, 'Er—you don't sound exactly overjoyed.'

There was a moment's silence at the other end, and when Desmond spoke, she knew he had made a conscious effort to pull himself together. 'I am, actually,' he said slowly. 'Thrilled, if the truth is known, that all the hard work has paid off and to know I've climbed another rung of the success ladder—but. . .' Georgina waited, and he added, the small spurt of enthusiasm going from his voice, 'I've been let down over a dinner engagement.' Another pause, then, 'I suppose you've already eaten?'

Such was their friendship that Georgina wasn't offended that she was being called in as second best. She knew very well what had happened. He had telephoned Lara at the first possible opportunity asking her to dine with him, Lara had agreed but, as she had been known to do before, had telephoned him at the last moment to say she couldn't make it. Her heart went out to him.

'Actually, Desmond, you're speaking to a girl who's literally starving. I missed my lunch today, so I could eat a horse.'

'Can you be ready in half an hour?' he asked. 'I've a table booked for half past eight.'

Georgina went into her bedroom after she had finished speaking with him. Knowing Desmond, he had probably booked a table at one of the plusher restaurants Lara preferred—the Bellington, she wouldn't mind betting; it was a favourite of Lara's. It looked like a case for the 'little black dress', she thought, extracting the black velvet dinner gown from her wardrobe. She'd had it ages. Desmond had seen it half a dozen times, but she was confident it suited her, and she always felt good in it. Its rounded neck line showed up her creamy skin, the fitted bodice moulded snugly to her curves.

Her mind went over her first meeting with Desmond as she had the quickest of baths. Because she couldn't allow herself to become seriously involved, she always saw to it that if she felt like dating any one man more than once, then dates were always spaced so that her escort should in no way gain the idea that they were going steady. And then she rarely dated the same man more than three times. She had met Desmond at a party, had liked the tall fair-haired man and had agreed to go out with him. Desmond hadn't told her until their third date that he was married, but by then the anger she had experienced at this news had been tempered by knowing something of the man himself. She had liked his quiet manner, felt comfortable with him, liked his air of maturity that he didn't, like so many men she was acquainted with, seem to think that because he took her out it meant he should be rewarded with at least a kiss at the end of the evening. Bluntly she had told him on that third date that she wouldn't go out with him again. Desmond had been prepared to accept that, though he had explained he wanted nothing from her but friendship, telling her it wasn't much fun being on his own.

Desmond telling her of his loneliness had brought back vividly how desperately lonely her father had been when her mother had left them, how desolate he had looked on the day of the divorce. His desolation had stayed with him and hadn't been helped by a succession of chilly housekeepers who had tramped through the house in Kenilworth.

But all that had changed that lovely, lovely day when the widowed Maggie had come to housekeep for them, bringing with her the three-year-old Nicola and Josh going on for six. It had been impossible to be glum with Maggie about and life had really picked up from then on. Her

father had married Maggie after a very short while and
their dreary existence was a thing of the past. Maggie had
filled the house with laughter. She had taught Georgina,
a solemn and withdrawn teenager, to laugh. She would
never forget Maggie's goodness to her. There had never
been very much money to spare, but Maggie had insisted
that she have the best secretarial training money could buy.
Father was dead now, and money was tighter than ever.
Nicola was fourteen and Josh nearly seventeen, and
Georgina saw it was up to her to do all she could to see
that Maggie's children had the same chance in life that
Maggie had insisted she should have.

Desmond would be here soon, Georgina thought, as she
applied a smear of lipstick to her mouth, her mind flitting
back to that chance meeting she had had with him and his
tentative suggestion that she dine with him. She had recalled then the thoughts she'd had on her father's loneliness, had wondered if she was being too hard on Desmond.
She had witnessed in his bleak eyes the same look that
had been in her father's eyes before Maggie had banished
it, and her mind was made up. Both she and Desmond had
gained something from their friendship. For on her side,
since marriage was out of the question anyway until Nicola
and Josh's future was settled, she had a very dear friend,
and if she could help him over this bad patch now that
Lara had gone back on her word to have dinner with him,
then she was pleased to do so.

'You're looking fit and well,' she said, when he arrived.
'Not been living it up too much?'

'My days have been spent battling over contracts, not
on holiday,' he assured her, rising to her teasing.

'And you pulled the deal off.'

Desmond nodded. 'Yes,' he said, 'and now I could sleep
for a week.'

'But not before you've fed your old comrade?'

He smiled at her. 'Thanks for agreeing to come at such short notice.' Lara's name wasn't mentioned, but with her understanding a little of Desmond's feelings, Georgina realised that his estranged wife backing out from their dinner engagement the way she had done had left him feeling bruised and in no mood for his own company.

As she had suspected, he had booked a table at the Bellington, and it was on the way there that some of his enthusiasm for his work began to show itself as he recounted some of the incidents of his negotiations. As always Georgina was interested in what he had to tell her, and decided her news of the takeover would keep until later, so she listened attentively while he outlined how things had gone, how at one stage he had thought he had lost, having had tough opposition, but how gradually things had worked back his way. Then he was parking his car and escorting her into the Bellington.

Georgina stood looking about her in the foyer while Desmond went to see about their table. She liked it here, though it was not very often she and Desmond dined in such expensive surroundings. She heard the whisper of the revolving door being pushed round, but had no particular interest in the new arrivals, her senses being concentrated on a delightful watercolour on the wall to the right of her. When her name was spoken, the voice vaguely familiar, she turned slowly, in no way prepared for the shock she would receive as she recognised not only the girl who had addressed her from the side, 'It is Georgina, isn't it?' but recognised also the man who was with her.

'Fancy seeing you here!' Lara Warner exclaimed. Then for the benefit of her escort, Georgina was sure, since Lara must know she was here with Desmond, Lara said in a subdued little voice, 'You're dining alone,'

'I'm here with Desmond,' Georgina told her, her voice coming out more short than she had meant it to. She had no wish to take sides in Desmond's marital problems, but she knew he was going to be dreadfully hurt to see Lara here when less than an hour ago she must have telephoned him to say she couldn't dine with him.

Lara gave her a sharp-eyed look, then adopted a hurt look as if to say it upset her that Desmond was Georgina's escort. And then the man who was with Lara was stepping in to relieve the taut atmosphere.

'How very nice to see you again, Georgina,' said Tallis York, with a sangfroid that almost took her breath away, considering the last time she had seen him he could have been in no doubt that she was furiously angry.

'I...' she began, but had no time for any more because she saw Desmond coming back. She saw his eyes light on Lara straight away. Saw the pain in his expression before he mastered it, and because she had some idea of his hurt, her smile was especially welcoming when he came up to them.

'Hello Lara—Tallis,' he said, with what Georgina thought was admirable restraint, as it registered with her that Desmond was already acquainted with Tallis York. Then like a drowning man clutching for something to hang on to, she felt his hand take hold of hers and grip on to it as though he needed some of her strength to help him collect himself together.

As Tallis York had witnessed the smile she had beamed across at Desmond, she saw his eyes go to their clasped hands. But regardless of what he thought, she saw from the way his left eyebrow went up, from the mocking look in his eyes, that he was as good as saying, 'Just good friends?' but she made no move to extricate her hand.

'Have you eaten?' Tallis asked conversationally.

'We're just about to,' Desmond told him.

'I know,' Lara put in to Georgina's amazement, 'why don't we all eat together?'

Desmond seemed as amazed as Georgina at Lara's suggestion. What Tallis York was feeling was anybody's guess, although he did look down at the petite Lara, and Georgina wondered whether it was to ascertain whether or not she was being serious.

'It's unlikely they'll have a table for four unreserved,' Georgina said, thinking that Desmond would rather do anything than have a cosy foursome that included Tallis York, even if he did know him. She remembered distinctly that night at the theatre when she had met Lara for the first time, he had been so jealous of the man who was escorting his wife he had barely said two words to him. Then as if she hadn't spoken, Tallis York was ignoring her and asking Desmond how he felt about the four of them joining up.

'It's all right by me,' Desmond agreed, and without waiting to see if Georgina had any objections to the idea, Tallis York went away to get things organised.

He was back in a very short while to say a table for four had been arranged. Georgina looked at him, tall, rugged, and really handsome in his dinner jacket, she thought begrudgingly. His air of authority had not been left behind with his business suit, she noted, as he looked back at her with those dark mocking eyes. She looked away; somehow she hadn't expected him to have any trouble in changing the arrangements.

The head waiter escorted them to their table, and Lara sat opposite Georgina, both girls with a man at each side. Lara was beautiful, Georgina thought, as she looked at the other girl and tried to fathom out exactly what game she was playing, though she thought she relied on make-up to make her mouth appear more generous than it was. She looked away from her, observing absently that a four-piece band was playing for those who wished to dance.

Talk was uncomplicated as their choices of meal was decided upon, Georgina conferring with Desmond over her selection. Then, the meal underway, Lara made some reference to travel, and Tallis was addressing Desmond.

'You've been in Belgium recently, Lara tells me?'

'Had some business to do over there,' Desmond replied.

'You got back today?' Lara asked, rather than stated, Georgina thought with surprise, half expecting him to tell Lara she knew very well he had.

'That's right,' he said briefly.

'And was your business successful?' she enquired.

Georgina had no idea what Desmond had revealed to his wife over the telephone, but with her sympathies all going out in his direction she thought that he might have been saving his good news until they were dining alone together. She couldn't help but feel sorry for him, especially when his reply was equally brief:

'Very.'

Then he addressed himself to Tallis, with a surprising lack of animosity, she thought, since she fully expected him to ignore anyone who escorted his wife other than himself.

'How's business with you, Tallis?' he asked.

'So-so,' Tallis replied. 'The market as it is today keeps us on our toes.'

'Your competitors would have to be up early in the morning to put one over on you,' Georgina heard Desmond opine, and thought she'd have to agree with him there, but she was more interested in how soon this meal would be over than to want to join them in any conversation that would probably be over her head anyway; already Desmond was going on to talk about one company who had recently folded under the pressure of the economic situation.

'If it's not go under, it's sell out these days,' Desmond was saying, reminding her that she hadn't yet had the chance to tell him anything about Chestertons taking over Parton and Naylor.

If Lara hadn't mentioned anything to him either during their phone conversation, then he would have no idea she was now dining out with the head of the firm that employed her. It was a funny old world, she thought without humour. This morning she had been verbally attacking his non-celibate state and this evening, when she had already planned never to put herself anywhere near him, she was having dinner in his company. And then, as though Lara had picked up her thoughts from a moment ago, she was joining in the conversation and saying to Desmond:

'Talking of selling out, you knew of course that Parton and Naylor had been taken over by Chestertons?'

Desmond's astonishment was obvious. 'No!' he exclaimed disbelievingly, his eyes going to Georgina. 'When? You never said anything, Georgina.'

Why she should feel guilty, Georgina didn't know. She could have told him, she supposed. He wasn't likely to go shouting it all over the city.

'Georgina is a true confidential secretary,' Tallis York said before she could say anything to excuse herself. If he had seen she was feeling uncomfortable under Desmond's wounded look, then he wasn't showing it. But his remark certainly got her over an awkward moment. Though she suspected his next remark was more than a little tongue in cheek when he added, 'We're most fortunate to have her on our staff.'

Not wanting to look at him to see the mocking look in his eyes that would belie the sincerity of his words, and still feeling a shade too guilty, for all she had only been doing her job, to look at Desmond, Georgina looked across at Lara, and was startled to see the other girl looking back at her with a look that could only be called venomous. Why, she thought, the composure she had clung on to all evening badly shaken by the look in the other girl's eyes, Lara wants me out as much as her father does. It was all too clear from Lara's look that she didn't agree with Tallis York's opinion that Chestertons were fortunate to have Georgina Underwood working for them. That look had told her that Lara Warner was pushing her father every step of the way to get her dismissed.

Panic that was growing familiar now gripped her as she realised the only person at Chestertons who could possibly hold out against Edgar Rankin was the chairman himself, Tallis York, and by being here tonight with Lara he was showing that he was very friendly with the prime instigator in the efforts to make one Georgina Underwood lose her job.

She felt his eyes on her, and pulled her gaze away from Lara to look at him. Would a man in his position bother to hold out regardless of the consequences to the workforce of Parton and Naylor under the persuasion of not only his girl-friend Lara, but also her father, a member of his board? she wondered as her eyes met night-black ones, that for once had lost their mockery.

CHAPTER THREE

How long she and Tallis York continued to look at each other in silence, Georgina never knew. Perhaps only seconds, she thought later. But she was aware that her air of sophistication had left her. She felt terribly vulnerable suddenly, and she knew that Tallis York was aware of it too. Those dark eyes pierced into her as though he was trying to see right into her very soul. Then he was turning to look at Lara, almost as if he had sensed something had gone on between the two of them. Then Desmond, whose attention had been taken up with spooning sugar into his coffee, looked up, completely oblivious of any byplay, and asked Tallis:

'You knew about Georgina before you met her this evening?'

Georgina's heart started to pound heavily. She wouldn't forget that look on Lara's face in a hurry, but there was a more immediate crisis pending just then. If Tallis York repeated anything of the accusation he had levelled at her today, she wasn't sure, even though Desmond would probably come off second best, that regardless of their surroundings, he wouldn't aim a fist at Tallis York's jaw.

'Actually,' she jumped in quickly before Tallis could say anything, 'I was over at Chestertons this afternoon. Mr York wanted to see some confidential papers rather urgently,' she explained her visit, prepared to lie her head off rather than tell Desmond what had taken place.

She waited for Tallis York to contradict her, knowing that even if he suspected Desmond might take a swing at him, it wouldn't bother him in the slightest if he didn't feel inclined to fall in with her lies. She turned her head to look at him, saw the mockery was back in his eyes in full force and that he was watching her.

He appeared to think the reason for her visit had been explained fully enough, she thought with relief, for he killed it stone dead by not agreeing or disagreeing with anything she had said, but told her:

'I may be your employer Georgina, but do you think just for tonight you could bring yourself to call me Tallis?'

It was the last thing she had expected him to say, and it caught her momentarily on the wrong foot, before she realised that perhaps it was a perfectly normal request since he was about the same age as Desmond, and this was a social occasion.

'Of course,' she said after a long second, but she didn't tack on his first name.

'Well, this is cosy,' said Lara, never one to allow herself to be left out of the conversation for very long, and sounding as though it wouldn't take very much for her to get bitchy.

'Isn't it, though,' said her husband a touch tightly.

Georgina wondered then if Desmond had any idea what Lara was up to. She herself was getting deeper and deeper into the fog of trying to understand what Lara was doing here with Tallis at the self-same restaurant as her and Desmond of all places. She watched the tight look disappear from his face to be replaced by a bleakness that revealed to her the pain inside him. When he glanced her way it was the most natural thing in the world to give him an encouraging smile.

'Dance, Georgina?'

Georgina's eyes abruptly left Desmond to find that Tallis York was rising to his feet, obviously the thought never crossing his mind that she would refuse. And such was the authority of the man, albeit in a velvet glove, that she found herself on her feet and going with him on to the dance area.

The quartet were playing a slow smoochy number that required Tallis to put an arm around her, and she felt that arm come round her securely like tempered steel, for all he did not pull her close to him. If she had hoped to complete the dance in absolute silence then before they had barely moved off, she found she was vastly mistaken, for Tallis York had one or two sharp and pertinent things to say to her, and the aggression she had witnessed earlier that day was out in full force as he said them.

'Can't you wait to get him home before you eat him?' he rapped at her.

His voice, in no way pleasant, jerked her own anger out of cold storage. 'Desmond?' she enquired shortly, trying to hold down her temper this man so easily aroused.

'Who else? You may be his mistress, but I would have thought good taste would have had you masking your desire to get him into bed while his wife is present.'

Oh, how she wished she'd told Desmond everything. Oh, what wouldn't she give to be able to deliver that punch on the jaw personally! Just because the brute of a man she was dancing with had caught her smiling at Desmond, he had read it as a signal that she was champing at the bit to get him back to her place.

'I've already told you,' she said tightly, meaning to count up to ten but not getting past five, 'that Desmond and I are nothing more than friends. We are not now, or ever have been, lovers, and if you could get your mind up off the floor, you'd believe me.'

'And if you'd seen as much of the world as I have, you'd know I'm not likely to swallow that tale,' Tallis York snapped back, his aggravation with her in no way hindering his dancing as he executed a perfect reverse turn she had no trouble following.

'Oh, believe what you want to, and damn you!' Georgina exploded. And, too het up suddenly to want to know what he thought of that, she rushed on furiously, 'And since you're such a man of the world I don't suppose you being here with Lara tonight will mean you'll be content to "just hold her hand" when you return her to her home tonight!'

Privately, Georgina thought that was rather a nasty thing to have said, but she didn't regret it. Why should he think he could say what he liked to her and not be repaid in kind? When he pulled back from her to look into her face, she half expected him to take her to task for that remark, but the angry look had gone from his face, and if anything, she thought the look on his face was one of puzzlement.

'Didn't you know Lara is my cousin?' he asked slowly. And when from the way Georgina just gaped at him he could see she had no idea, he told her, 'Edgar Rankin is my mother's brother, our two families have always been very close.'

The tune the band were playing came to an end, but Tallis didn't take his arm away from her as she just stood and looked at him. And then the musicians struck up again and once more they were dancing, still to a slow smoochy tune.

'I had no idea,' said Georgina, as what he had just told her began to penetrate.

Tallis was silent as he guided her in time to the music, and her spirits plummeted. She had thought she was going to have a battle on her hands to keep her job now that she knew Lara was the instigator behind the move to get her out. But what chance did she have of keeping it now she knew Lara was not any casual girl-friend, but a member of his family? They'd always been very close, he had said. She recalled Tallis telling her that he strongly objected to being petitioned at every opportunity to get rid of her. He had said then that 'for other reasons' he found himself having to put up with it. Instinctively she knew then that those 'other reasons' were his family ties. Where someone in his position might be able to say 'No' and mean it, members of one's family were specially privileged, and that 'No' was there to be worked on.

'Lara wants me out too, doesn't she?' she asked, following her own line of thought, but finding he had no trouble in keeping up with her.

'That's hardly surprising, is it?'

So they were back to that mistress thing again? It was a waste of breath to repeat what she had already said, Georgina thought. She could deny it until she was blue in the face and he wasn't going to believe her.

'Lara left Desmond, not the other way around,' she protested.

'No woman of Lara's temperament is going to hang around when her husband starts straying,' she was informed heavily.

'But . . .' Georgina began, ready to tell him she was sure Desmond was so much in love with his wife that the thought of straying, as he put it, had never entered his head. And then cold shock hit her before she could continue, as it dawned on her that what Tallis York was actually saying was that she and Desmond had been having an affair even before Lara had left him. 'Now wait a minute . . .' she started to say, feeling her temper fraying again and about to tell him in no uncertain terms that Lara had left Desmond three months before she had even met him. But before she could say more, Tallis York was biting into her.

'No, you wait a minute. It's obvious to me that Lara

regrets having left her husband. Equally obvious to me is the fact that she wants to go back to him ...'

'What makes it so obvious to you that Lara wants to go back to him?' Georgina asked, refusing to be quiet. She just didn't believe him. Lara could go back to Desmond anytime she wanted to, and she knew it. If she wasn't so pigheaded about wanting to see her husband on the board of Chestertons she could ...

'She couldn't wait to see him tonight for one thing,' said Tallis, causing Georgina to know he had no idea Lara had already turned down Desmond's invitation to do that very thing. 'I had occasion to ring Lara's father this evening over a small matter. When I'd finished my conversation with Edgar, Lara came on the line saying she felt low and would I take her out to dinner. I didn't think anything of it as Lara has often asked me to take her out in the past when she's been a bit fed up. I know Lara pretty well,' he went on, 'and as soon as I saw you, I suspected Warner wouldn't be far away. When Lara suggested the four of us should join up, I knew then exactly why she'd chosen the Bellington for our meal—like I said, she couldn't wait to see him.'

Georgina had listened to what Tallis had told her, and was about to reveal that she couldn't understand his theory about Lara wanting to see Desmond because he had been in touch with Lara before she had spoken to Tallis and asked him to take her to dinner. But then she saw something he hadn't seen, couldn't have seen, because Lara hadn't seen fit to tell him that Desmond had already been in touch with her. And she knew then exactly what game Lara was playing.

Lara might well want to see Desmond as Tallis had said, she conceded, and in her view Lara wanted a slipper administering where it hurt most for giving Desmond the runaround if that was the case. But Georgina had seen where Tallis couldn't possibly, since he didn't know about the prior arrangements and his cousin's subsequent cancellation of them, that Lara had seen a splendid chance of killing two birds with one stone. She had known Desmond would book a table at the Bellington, he had in all probability told her he would, and Lara had guessed when she rang back and said she couldn't make it, that he would bring her. By coming here with Tallis, Lara had ensured that not only would she see Desmond, but she had also ensured that the chairman would believe that the only person Desmond couldn't wait to see when he got back was one Georgina Underwood and that he had not given a thought to his wife. Lara had lost no time making the point, 'You got back today?' Making it look as though she hadn't known, and underlining that Georgina Underwood came first in her husband's thoughts.

It was a shock to know that Lara wanted her dismissed from Chestertons so badly she could stoop to such lengths. Georgina could see then the emotional blackmail Lara would bring to bear, remembered Lara's assumed look of hurt in the foyer, and knew then there was not the remotest chance of getting Tallis York to believe she and Desmond were nothing more than friends.

'So you think Lara is still in love with Desmond?' she asked, having no intention of putting forward her theory just to have it disbelieved and scoffed at.

'I'm sure of it.'

Tallis swung her round so she could see the table where Lara and Desmond were sitting. To her amazement she saw that they were laughing at something one or other of them had said, and looking for all the world as though no one else existed outside their two selves. Then Tallis was guiding her so she could no longer see them, though she was sure it wasn't because he thought it might be too painful for her to watch.

'Can't you leave him alone, girl?' She heard his voice above her head. It was neither cold nor mocking, and as she tried to decipher exactly what his voice was conveying, like being struck by a thunderbolt she realised it was pity.

Pity! she thought, astounded. Then, good grief, he thinks I'm in love with Desmond and that seeing them together like that has upset me! He could have no idea it was one of her dearest wishes that Lara would return to Desmond and that Desmond would be happy again.

The band were playing the last few bars, and the music came to an end. Georgina had not spoken since Tallis had told her to leave Desmond alone, but as she would have moved out of the semi-circle of his arm, she felt that arm close hard to her waist refusing to let her go. She looked up and saw that any pity she had heard in his voice was now a thing of the past.

'Let him go, Georgina,' he urged. 'Without you around there might yet be a chance for them to reconcile their differences.'

Georgina wanted to snatch herself out of his hold, but didn't want anyone to witness an ungainly struggle if he was determined to hang on to her. Was there a chance of a reconciliation? she wondered, suddenly fed up with the lot of them, Desmond included. Far be it from her to be the spanner in the works.

'All right,' she snapped, never having seen herself as 'the other woman' and sickened by the picture Tallis York was painting. 'Lara can have her chance with Desmond. And since you've suddenly turned into a boy scout and feel the urge to do your good deed for the day—you can take me home.' She was speaking without thinking, disliking intensely the whole sordid mess. 'And since you're

the genius,' she added, 'you can think of something to tell
Desmond.'

'My God, you're sure of him!' exclaimed Tallis, letting
go his hold on her, a sharp, calculating look coming over
his face. 'Or is it,' he said to her added fury, 'that you see
me as a much bigger fish to get your hooks into?'

How she kept the lid on her rage, Georgina just didn't
know, but she managed it, just. 'I'm sure you take your
running shoes with you wherever you go,' she replied
sweetly, and not caring if he was following her or not, she
went back to their table.

Never having expected Tallis to pick up the gauntlet that
in the heat of her temper she had so rashly thrown down,
she was astonished, before she could even take her seat, to
feel his hand on her arm staying her as he told Desmond
that he was taking her home.

How she covered her amazement Georgina didn't know
as she heard Tallis carrying on from the lie that she had
begun; that she had inadvertently taken the papers she
had taken for him to see late that afternoon back with her.
Wasn't it providential that he should see her here tonight,
he was telling Desmond with that easy assurance of his, for
he had discovered while dancing with Georgina that with
it being too late for her to return to her office, the papers
he needed for an early meeting tomorrow morning were
back in Georgina's home.

Georgina just didn't know how she kept her mouth
from dropping open as Tallis delivered his oh, so plausible
little speech—she thought it was nothing short of brilliant
when he ended:

'You don't mind seeing Lara home for me, do you?'
Which even if Desmond did mind, and she knew he didn't,
then without appearing extremely ungallant, there was just
no way he could make any protest.

'O.K.,' said Georgina once she was seated beside Tallis heading towards her apartment; Lara and Desmond had not looked at all put out that partners had been switched when they had left them, 'so now we know you're a genius.'

She hadn't meant her remark to sound flattering, and it certainly hadn't come out sounding anything other than sarcastic, but Tallis York wasn't in any way bothered by her sarcasm.

'Modesty forbids me from agreeing with you,' he said urbanely.

And never had Georgina felt more like hitting a man. For the rest of the drive she kept her comments solely on giving him directions to where she lived.

'Do I get to come in?' Tallis asked as, the car stationary, the engine switched off, he parked outside the entrance to the house that had been converted into flats.

Georgina didn't bother answering knowing he would draw from that her answer was a definite no, and also that she had no intention of getting into an argument with him about it. Though why he should want to see inside her flat she couldn't think.

She was appalled to find he had read her non-reply as yes, for not even deigning to say goodnight to him, a politeness her conscience might have pricked her about tomorrow if it had had the chance, she found he had left his car and was going up the concrete steps to the main door with her. She took a deep breath in an effort to control her rising ire, inserted her key inside the big front door, and turned to say a dismissive goodnight, only to find he had pushed the door wide and was helping her through, finding the light switch and closing the door behind them.

'Goodnight, Mr York,' she tried anyway, her face unsmiling.

'I'll see you to your door,' he replied coolly, with the air of a man who thought it the height of bad manners to do anything other, and Georgina felt her key ring being taken from her hand as Tallis gave her a look that said, 'Lead on.'

Only just saving herself from making a grab for her keys—she doubted he would have released them anyway and she had no intention of grappling for them—she led the way to the first floor where her small flat was situated, and stood quietly seething as Tallis York opened her door, then stood back to let her precede him.

Their hands reached the light switch together. She felt the tingle of his touch as light flooded her sitting room, and went to drop her hand away from his, only to find he wasn't ready to let her hand go. He closed the door and, still holding her hand, looked round her neat and tidy room with its one easy chair, comfortable-looking settee, and the bits and pieces she had gathered around her in the years she had been living there.

'May I have my hand back?' she asked, striving desperately for her sophisticated air that in no way matched the feeling that was growing inside her that any sophistication she had was becoming wobbly when Tallis York's eyes went deliberately to her mouth.

Oh God, don't let him start anything, she thought, and couldn't be sure suddenly whether her fear was because the threat of her dismissal would come even closer if she had to hit him if he did try anything, or because there was something about the way he was looking at her; that look telling her he was rarely, if ever, refused in these matters, that had her traitorous thoughts wondering against all her inclinations what it would be like to be kissed by him.

'Such a lovely hand,' he answered, not complying with her request to release it, but instead bringing it up to inspect it before taking it to his mouth where his lips lightly brushed across the back of it.

Undignified or not, Georgina tried to pull her hand away. She was feeling strange flames of excitement flickering into life inside her that were unwanted and even less understood as he refused to let go, but instead was taking advantage of his hold to pull her nearer to him.

'I . . . I think you should go now, Mr York,' she said, and hated that her voice wasn't sounding as forceful as she had meant it to sound.

'Tallis,' he corrected her. 'Your lovely face matches your lovely hand, Georgina.' He gave another tug and she was forced to go that step nearer that brought their two bodies almost up against each other.

'Look, Mr Y—Tallis,' she said, aware that her voice had become husky, but unable to do anything about it because those dark eyes glittering close to hers were having an hypnotic affect on her.

'Shh!' said Tallis softly, then what she had been expecting, wanting some part of her mind seemed to say, was happening, and Tallis York was bending his head towards her mouth. Feeling she just had to make some protest, her lips parted, and that was as far as she got, for his mouth met hers and Georgina knew she had never been kissed by an expert before.

She tried to fight against the longing to yield to him, unable to understand why she had to make the effort consciously when it should come automatically. But as his arms came round her and he gathered her to him, she had the hardest work in the world not to give in.

She felt his fingers running along her spine, and couldn't help but clutch at him as a tremor of delight shot through her. As the pressure on her mouth increased, her arms went up and around him and she knew she just wasn't thinking any more; he was arousing a reaction in her body over which she had no control.

His mouth left hers briefly, as his lips sought her throat with a persuasion that make her legs feel weak. Then he was pulling her hard to him, moulding her body to his, and as a shudder of exquisite delight shot through her, some of her natural sensitivity and reticence argued with the wantonness of her feelings, and the girl she had always known herself to be drew back, afraid of where all this was leading.

'Forget Warner,' Tallis breathed in her ear, misunderstanding her action.

Hearing Desmond's name, for all there had never been anything like this between them, had her senses unscrambling themselves as the remarks Tallis had made on the dance floor roared to be heard. 'My God, you're sure of him,' he had said, and had followed that remark up with, 'Or is it that you see me as a much bigger fish to get your hooks into?'

Was that what this was all about? Did he think her careless challenge for him to take her home so that Desmond could have some time alone with Lara meant he thought she wouldn't mind dropping Desmond for bigger pickings? And if he did think that, then why, with his eyes wide open, was he showing every sign of going along with her? Oh, his virility had never been in doubt, but she couldn't see that virility ruling his head if he knew he was being taken for a ride.

These thoughts rattled through Georgina's head, to come to a dead stop as she felt his fingers at the zipper of her dress, his touch so skilled she hadn't been aware her zip had moved until she felt the cool air on her naked skin and she knew her zip must be half way down her back. And then she froze.

'You can just do that back up,' she said coldly, her hands coming away from him.

Immediately Tallis stilled, pulled back so he could see into her face. Her icy expression left him knowing she meant what she said.

'As my lady pleases,' he shrugged, pulling up her zip, and there was that mocking look in his eyes that let her know, to her chagrin, that while he had made her pulses race so that she thought her heart would be overloaded, his seduction of her had been attempted with a very cool head.

'My apologies, Georgina,' he said, the way he said it an insult since he was showing clearly that whatever effect he had on her, the effect she had on him had not even smeared a mist of cloud on his precise thinking. 'It appears my brand of lovemaking is not what you're used to.'

She didn't doubt that that was yet another dig at what he thought went on between her and Desmond, and anger merged with hurt, and had her saying recklessly:

'That's true enough. I *am* used to a certain—finesse ...'

Anything else she might have added was lost as she saw all mockery die from his face. She had meant to hurt him, and knew her barb, the use of that word 'finesse', had bit.

'Maybe I wasn't as subtle as I usually am on these occasions,' he conceded, and if he was angry then his anger was closely tethered, 'but with you giving me the go-ahead when you invited me to take you home—given you tried your hand at the hard-to-get treatment when we stopped inside the front door—I thought I was home and dry, subtleties not needed. But finesse or not, you wouldn't have objected too much had I not reminded you that Warner looks like being a better long-term investment than myself.'

Never was she more glad she had stopped him when she had. He was making no bones about telling her he would soon tire of anything she had to offer. She was doubly glad she had stopped him, especially when he added:

'Had I not reminded you of your commitment to him things would have worked out very differently. Your bedmate wouldn't have been a married man tonight.'

If she had intended to wound him with her barb about his lack of finesse, his cold reprobation of her and what he thought were her morals, Georgina found far more wounding. Particularly as that was the very first time she had forgotten herself so far as to actually want a man. That he could be so contemptuous of her made her feel quite ill. And then she saw quite clearly the answer to what a few minutes before had been puzzling her. The answer to why, if Tallis thought she was prepared to let their lovemaking go to its ultimate conclusion, was he then allowing himself to be used, thinking as he did she was after a man who outclassed Desmond in worldly possessions. The answer to that was suddenly startlingly clear. She saw him walk casually to the door and knew that having said his piece he was ready to leave.

'You were trying to cut Desmond out, weren't you?' she accused as he reached the door. 'You thought if I went to bed with you then all you had to do was to tell Desmond tomorrow, and as soon as he knew, our affair would be finished.'

Tallis turned round, and if he had been angry before then he wasn't angry any longer. 'But you're not having an affair with Warner, are you?' he mocked. 'Surely you and he are just good friends?'

The sick feeling Georgina had taken with her to bed was still with her when she awakened the next morning. Vividly she recalled again the scene that had taken place between her and Tallis last night. She had hoped the memory of her own feelings would have faded after a few hours' sleep, but found she was out of luck as again she wondered what had come over her.

There was nothing about the man to like. She had always thought when the time came that the man she felt she wanted to give herself to arrived, then that man would be kind, loving and gentle. She had thought that feeling of wanting to stay in his arms and experience more, would only arrive when she had known the man in question for some time, had learnt to know something about him, and that their mutual regard for each other would slowly, gradually have grown to that moment when a mutual love would take its natural course. Tallis York, a man she had known for less than twelve hours, a man who was neither kind, loving nor gentle, had taken her in his arms, and shatteringly had turned every one of her theories upside down.

And what about *her own* body? What about her own reactions? She got out of bed and hurried around her flat getting ready to go to the office and trying to escape her thoughts. But there was no escaping them. They nudged her elbow as she bathed, dressed, and ate her toast. Had that really been her last night? She choked on a mouthful of too-hot coffee and had a brief moment of respite from the torment of her thoughts before they crowded in on her again. The emotions she had felt last night had been wildly outside her previous experience. Oh, she had been kissed before, had kissed back, but always with a certain reserve. Not for her the casual hopping in and out of bed. It wasn't in her nature, or so she'd thought.

She broke out into a cold sweat as her thoughts went on. What if Tallis hadn't taken no for an answer? What if he had piled on his undoubted expertise and drowned her protests, intensified his lovemaking—all her previously held beliefs had crumbled without resistance before the

natural reticence in her had made itself felt—but what if
he had managed to overcome her reticence, what then?
He'd be laughing himself silly this morning! He would
have learnt by then that she had been speaking the truth
when she had told him she wasn't Desmond's mistress; he
would have learned she had never been any man's mistress.

Glad to be at her office with something to do to keep her
thoughts from straying back to something she considered
she had given more than enough time to, Georgina concentrated hard on the job on hand for the first half an hour
until the phone rang.

'Ah, Georgina,' said the voice at the other end, belonging to the man who had taken up far too many of her
thoughts in the short time she had known him. Then when
she hadn't found her voice, 'Gone to sleep on me?' mocked
that hated voice.

Georgina swallowed hastily, striving for her best secretarial image, and said coolly, 'Good morning, Mr York.' It
had been Tallis last night, she recalled, her hastily gathered
control slipping before she grabbed it back. 'Can I help
you?' she offered evenly, when it seemed he was taking
his time in coming to the point, determined to keep a
hold on her control, though if he had telephoned merely
to have another dig at her friendship with Desmond, then
regardless that he had the power to throw her out on her
ear, she didn't trust herself not to send the phone crashing
down.

'I'm sure you could,' came the sardonic tones, followed
by a pause as he waited for that two-edged statement to
sink in. Her mouth firmed into a tight line, then her lips
almost fell open as he went on, 'Get over here as soon as
you can, there's a good girl.'

Oh God, was she never going to lose this anxiety of
being dismissed? 'What for?' she asked the Chairman of

Chestertons, fully realising that he never expected to have his orders questioned.

'I could tell you because I say so, but because you probably have a few loose ends you'll want to clear up there, since you won't be returning...'

Not returning! As those words penetrated, all Georgina's attempts to hold on to her control fled. So agitated did her feelings become at knowing she wouldn't be returning to Parton and Naylor, she jumped in before he could finish.

'If you think I'm coming across the city just so that you can tell me I've been dismissed, you can think again, Mr York!' She wasn't thinking any longer, words were just pouring out from her. 'And I can tell you this, that I don't think much of your company no matter how big it is, that you can so easily break your word to Mr Parton and get rid of one of his employees the minute his back is turned!' She was almost spitting with fury. This was the man who had held her in his arms last night—it sickened her anew than any man could so easily arouse that wantonness in her that she had never ever suspected she possessed and less than twelve hours later throw her out of her job. The nausea of her thoughts, combined with panic at not being able to meet her commitment to Maggie, had her not giving any thought at all to the fact that nobody spoke this way to Tallis York, ever. 'And I think less than nothing of you, Tallis York,' she raged, 'that you can be so weak-willed as to give in to pressure, unfair pressure I might add, from your relations who haven't even the decency to confront me personally.' About to add that she wouldn't consider working for his outfit for another minute even if he doubled her salary, she was stopped before she could say another word by a voice that fairly thundered down the line.

'Shut up!' he roared, and without waiting to hear whether she had or not, he enunciated very clearly, 'One more word out of you and I bloody well *will* sack you!'

'You mean ...' Georgina whispered, her voice dying with her temper as, his roaring rage aside, it looked from what he was saying as though it hadn't been his intention to dismiss her.

'Shut up and listen! I told you yesterday you would be Vincent Dixon's secretary when he returned if that was what you wanted, and regardless of family pressures, I shall not go back on my word. Now clear up everything you have outstanding there, and get over here.'

'But,' Georgina felt bound to insert, her brain seeming incapable of thinking for itself under the chilling anger coming at her from Tallis York, 'Why do ...'

'If you'd allowed me to tell you before you gave vent to abusing my character, I was about to tell you,' he said icily. 'We're short-staffed here—you'll be working where I can keep my eye on you for a while.'

'Working ...?' she began, but didn't get any further.

'*Move!*' Tallis York bellowed, and slammed the phone down.

Was he mad? Oh dear, he was *furious*! Georgina had been livid herself, she recalled as she replaced her phone, and tried to remember everything she had said to him. Had she really told him she didn't think much of Chestertons? Had she really told him she thought less than nothing of him? She didn't want to remember any more, but blamed him thoroughly for disturbing the even tenor of her emotions the way he had done last night. She had been ready to fly at him, in self-vindication against the desire he had aroused in her last night, she supposed. But oh, if only she had waited to hear him out first. Had she really called him weak-willed? That man who was strong enough not to yield to being got at by two members of the family he had already told her were close to him.

CHAPTER FOUR

'CLOSE the door, Georgina, would you,' Tallis York instructed her as she was shown into his office a little while later. 'Take a seat,' he further instructed, then, 'You made good time. I had thought we might not see you until this afternoon.'

'You said "move",' she reminded him, then oh, how she wished she hadn't, because it brought that telephone conversation slap bang into the open.

'Ah yes,' he said smoothly. 'And you, I believe, said a hell of a lot more.'

His voice was still civil, but only just. His tone was quiet, but she suspected an underlying iron in that tone that matched the steel in his eyes. She knew then that she wasn't going to be let off lightly.

'I did rather fall before I was pushed, didn't I?' she said carefully. As an apology it didn't even begin, but it was as far as she was prepared to go.

'You could say that,' he commented. 'You could make a better job of your apology too.'

She could hear the iron in his voice coming nearer to the surface, but when she knew full well it would be better for her to give him the unreserved apology he not only deserved, but seemed to be pressing for, some quirk in her nature refused to make it.

'Does it hurt you to say sorry?' he enquired. 'Or is it that you *do* believe I'm—what was it—weak-willed and a breaker of promises?'

Georgina knew he was playing cat and mouse with her.

He hadn't forgotten one single word she had said to him. He was just repeating it to try and make her squirm. Well, he didn't know Georgina Underwood very well, she'd be damned if she'd squirm at his bidding.

'It doesn't hurt me to say sorry, any more than it would hurt you, I shouldn't think,' she stated with a coolness that in no way matched her trembly insides.

'You're suggesting I owe you an apology? For what?' he asked, mockery mingling with the steel in his eyes, making him appear devilish to her at that moment. 'I think we established yesterday that you're no stranger to receiving kisses from the adult male,' he continued, to Georgina's horror going along a track she hadn't meant he should go along. 'Should I apologise for making you forget Warner for a brief while? Should I apologise for making you forget yourself?'

'Forget myself?' she echoed, swallowing hard.

'Are you saying you didn't?'

'That's not the point in question,' Georgina said with all the firmness she could muster, not wanting to have her feelings of last night taken out and openly analysed. She had done more than enough self-analysis in private, she could do without hearing what he had made of her pliant response, brief though it had been. 'That little episode of last night,' she added with all the offhandedness at her command, 'I think we can both put down to experience.'

Mockery had gone. There was pure steel only in his eyes when she looked at him to see how he had received her remark. 'So you're not asking for an apology for my lack of finesse?' She really had stung him with that one, hadn't she, Georgina thought. 'So if it isn't that, what then, Georgina, have I to apologise for?'

'You know damn well,' she snapped, and bit her lip as the words left her with a hastiness that showed him all too clearly that she was not feeling as calm as she was trying to appear. 'When you're ready to apologise to me for all the vile accusations you threw at me yesterday, for all the things you've said, for all the things you believe, then I'll give you a ...'

'You're still maintaining that you and Warner are nothing more than friends?'

She didn't answer him; she saw no point. They had been over all this before. Then while she was sitting there thinking how hopeless it all was—she desperate to keep her job, Tallis York being fired on by two sides to get her dismissed, probably being told daily of the iniquities of one Georgina Underwood—he leaned back in his chair, looked every inch of a man more than capable of making up his own mind without the help of his uncle and cousin, and said consideringly:

'I'll admit a couple of the things that happened last night gave me food for thinking maybe you're not as pally with Warner as would appear on the surface.'

Straightaway Georgina's spirits lifted. She wasn't sure why it should bother her that Tallis York might be beginning to doubt his previously held views about her. Possibly, she thought, because to have him believing her would have him on her side, and since there was no fault to be found with her work, any pressure Edgar Rankin brought to bear on Tallis could be argued against. But there was only a hint that Tallis might be persuaded to believe her, so before she started breathing any sighs of relief at having the smear taken from her character, she had better find out what he had witnessed last night to put the doubt in his mind in the first place.

'You said a couple of things happened ...' she probed when he wasn't forthcoming, and not being able to think of anything herself that might have worked towards him changing his opinion. He had construed the warm smile she had sent Desmond's way as meaning that she couldn't wait for the evening to end so she could have him all to herself, she recalled.

'Were you as thick with Warner as I had supposed, then confidential secretary or not, I think it likely you would have told him about the proposed takeover my group were planning for Parton and Naylor. Forgive me for being blunt,' he added, showing some of the finesse to her sensitivities she had accused him of not having, 'but there's many a boardroom secret that has been leaked in bed.' He didn't wait to see whether she had forgiven his bluntness or not, but went on. 'On the debit side,' he continued in his forthright way, and not sparing her as he outlined his conclusions, 'you had no idea of Lara's family connections with this firm, or the fact that she is my cousin. That in itself would seem to confirm that you are Warner's mistress, since only an idiot would go into details of his wife's family connections with the woman he's bedding. Few mistresses would appreciate their lover bringing anything to do with the wife into any discussion they had, and Warner is far from being an idiot.'

'It seems to me from what you've said that the one cancels out the other,' said Georgina, knowing she had been right not to give a sigh of relief too early. 'You still believe what you accused me of, and nothing I say or your own observations will make you think otherwise.' He could run for his apology, she thought, suddenly fed up.

'It would seem I have to,' Tallis admitted. 'And yet there was something about the way you unprotestingly let me take you home that had me thinking later that perhaps you might want Lara and Warner to become reconciled.'

'Even though you thought at the time I made the suggestion that I was sure Lara was no competition?' Georgina put in. Then, an edge creeping into her voice as she recalled what else he had said, 'Even though you thought I was after bigger pickings? You were quite blunt then too, as I recall. You said outright that you thought I might be after you.'

'The thought did cross my mind,' he agreed, and if she had thought she might unseat some of his colossal confidence by reminding him of it, she saw his confidence wasn't even dented. 'But you let me down badly, Georgina. You didn't play the game according to the rules. You called a halt when things looked like becoming—interesting.'

Georgina decided she didn't want to return to that subject. Though she could have done without the need to give a small cough to clear her throat before she next spoke.

'Yes—well,' she said, 'er—that's neither here nor there, is it? I have your word, haven't I, that my job is secure and everything else is beside the . . .'

'You believe in my word?' Tallis asked quietly.

And because she did, when she had firmly decided during this interview that she wasn't going to give him more of an apology than she had done, she found herself answering:

'Yes, yes, I do, and . . . and I'm sorry I said all those terrible things to you this morning. My only excuse is that this job means a lot to me.' She had spoken hurriedly, once started on her apology, wanting to get it said and over with, and realising too late she had said more than she had intended. She hoped Tallis wasn't going to ask her why her job should mean such a lot to her, because she had no intention of telling him, especially since it was more the salary she received that was important to her, much as she liked the work involved.

He didn't ask why her job meant so much to her—he

probably thought she was career-minded, she thought, but if she had been hoping for a reciprocal apology she didn't get that either. For it seemed he wasn't yet ready to apologise. It therefore followed, she thought, that though there might be a doubt in his mind that she might not be Desmond's mistress, Tallis hadn't by any long chalk swung over to believing completely in the innocence of her friendship with his cousin's husband.

'You enjoyed the work you did for Mr Parton?' he enquired instead.

'Very much,' she replied honestly, and watched while a look crossed his face that was definitely devilish. There was no mistaking it this time, she thought, as she waited with the suspicion growing within her that she wasn't going to like what he said next, whatever it was.

'In that case, let us hope you enjoy equally the work you will be doing for me.'

'You mean the work I shall be doing in this building?' she asked, needing clarification, not liking at all the look in his eyes and wanting only to get out of his office so that Mrs Fry could direct her to the department she had been assigned to.

'No,' said Tallis, and she was positive he was thoroughly enjoying himself at her expense. 'Mrs Fry was taken into hospital yesterday with peritonitis. I find myself temporarily without a secretary.' He paused as if savouring the next moment, his eyes intent on her. 'You, Georgina, have been elected to fill the breech.'

'But—but——' she stammered, knowing she was gaping foolishly as it sank in. Her! Secretary to the chairman of Chestertons! Seeing a man she reminded herself she had no liking for, every day! 'But surely you have other secretaries you can call on?' she protested.

'True,' said Tallis York, extracting every ounce of

pleasure from her gaping countenance. Oh, where was her sophistication now when she so badly needed it? 'But as I said on the phone, Georgina, I want you where I can see you.'

And before she could begin to know what to make of that, or even start to tell him that working as personal and confidential secretary to Mr Parton just didn't begin to compare with the high executive world Tallis York was pushing her into, he was getting out of his chair and instructing her to follow him into the office last occupied by Mrs Fry.

Georgina went home that night having gleaned a little of what being secretary to a chairman of a concern as big as Chestertons meant. She thought she had acquitted herself fairly well, but had to confess that after just one afternoon of fending off phone calls that seemed to be put through to her every other minute the moment Tallis had gone to a meeting, not counting the correspondence she had typed back from the tapes he had recorded in the absence of a secretary before she had got there, she felt positively whacked.

She lingered over her meal that night, needing the time to re-charge her batteries. Then, her healthy mind and body recovered, she set about doing a few bits of washing, her mind going over the events of the day.

She concentrated her thoughts on Desmond; Tallis York had taken up too much of her time. She should have thought out the Desmond situation last night, but the discovery about herself when Tallis had kissed her had sent every other thought out of her head. But now she had some serious thinking to do.

What was it Tallis had said? That without her around there might be a chance Lara and Desmond would reconcile their differences? It was a terrible thought, if it was true, that it was she who had prevented them getting back together again. But she couldn't believe it, could she? She hated Tallis York for putting that doubt in her mind. If Lara was still in love with Desmond as Tallis had been so certain she was, then in her view she had a mighty peculiar way of showing it. There had been at least three occasions in the last six months when Desmond had been like a dog with two tails because Lara had agreed to go out with him, then his joy had turned to despair because at the last moment she had cried off.

Georgina recalled how happy Lara and Desmond had looked together last night. Perhaps she was getting worked up over nothing, she thought, recalling that she had half expected a call from Desmond today—Parton's would have told him where she was—half expected him to want to share his good news, if not perhaps to tell her Lara had gone back to him, then perhaps to say things were looking a little rosier; after all, he so often rang her up when he was down, it would be nice to hear from him when he was up. But he hadn't rung, and that didn't sound too hopeful, she thought, and went back to the tangle of her thoughts.

More of what Tallis had said came back to her. He was definitely under the impression that his cousin had left Desmond because of her. Now who could have given him that impression? Had Lara, or perhaps her father, told him she had enticed Desmond while Lara still lived with him in order to use that as another lever to get Georgina dismissed? They both wanted her out, that was for sure. She wouldn't forget that look on Lara's face last night in a hurry.

Sick though she was feeling that her innocent friendship with Desmond was being construed in some quarters as very far from innocent, and not liking at all that she was suddenly piggy in the middle, Georgina saw that she had a very real problem before her. Just supposing, and she wasn't ready yet to fully believe it, but just supposing Tallis was right and that her being friends with Desmond *was* preventing Lara from going back to him, then there was no question but that friendship must cease.

Before she went to bed, Georgina considered ringing Desmond before she decided against it. If he was halfway to getting back with Lara then no good would come of her stirring up a hornets' nest by telling him everything Tallis had said to her.

She went to bed early, but almost got up again as the idea struck her of looking up Edgar Rankin's number and ringing Lara. That idea too was rejected as she pulled the bedclothes up over her head. Having met Lara a time or two, she was confident Lara didn't believe she was Desmond's mistress, and anyway Lara would soon have tackled Desmond if there was a shadow of doubt. Desmond would soon assure her in no uncertain terms that that definitely wasn't so. Georgina closed her eyes, her mind reeling from its constant questioning and elimination. She'd better get some sleep, she had to put in a full day at Chestertons tomorrow.

The next morning, from the moment she entered the office which was to be her place of work until Mrs Fry returned, she had little time to think of anything but the job in hand. Tallis York came in at nine-thirty, throwing her a businesslike, 'Good morning Georgina,' as he went through to his own office. She would have preferred that he had closed his office door after him. But when he could have done no more than empty out the contents of his briefcase on to his desk, he called, 'Come in, would you,' she saw why he had left his door open.

It had been open when she had arrived that morning, and she had seen then that the surface of his desk was clear, but now as she went in, she saw that file after file reposed there, and she could see from that that if he had been out on the town last night, then he must have gone to bed very late to have completed the work he had before he had turned in.

Her eyes left his desk, to find his dark eyes studying her. She didn't think he could find any fault with her appearance, for she took care of her clothes, and the navy trouser suit she wore that revealed the long length of her legs was well fitting. Embarrassed suddenly that he seemed in no hurry to cease his study of her, she said the first thing that came into her head.

'You couldn't have got to bed very early last night,' she said, her eyes leaving his to go once more to the mound of paper work on his desk.

Deliberately, she was sure, Tallis chose to misunderstand her. 'Oh, I wouldn't say that,' he said, still on that same mocking note. Then again deliberately, 'Regretting it wasn't you, Georgina?'

Her mouth almost dropped open as she followed the line of his thinking. Then, her lips firming, she looked at him, saw his eyes were alight with devilment, and had the urge to hit him. 'How fortunate for you that some of your —friends—are better acquainted with the rules than I myself,' she said sweetly.

'Oh, you know the rules all right,' he told her. 'Even though you're not above cheating a little.'

Georgina's hands clenched down by her sides. That was a direct reference to the fact that he thought her cheating to play the game with a married man. 'I was referring to the amount of work you must have got through last night,' she said coldly, needing all her will power not to hit him regardless of the consequences.

'Ah yes, work,' said Tallis, seeing she was resolved not

to be drawn further, and tiring of the game. 'Let's get down to it, we've a lot to get through today. Did you bring your notepad in?'

She hadn't. 'You're not going to tape your dictation?'

'You *can* take shorthand?' he asked in reply.

Unspeaking, she went and got her notepad, chiding herself for not thinking before she spoke. She had seen Mrs Fry that first morning transcribing from shorthand, she remembered now; that should have told her Tallis didn't always use the dictaphone.

Later in the morning he went out telling her he might not be back until she was at lunch, and instructing her that any messages she had for him she could leave on tape, and he would play them back.

Glad to be on her own, finding she was too new at the job to forget completely his presence in the next door office, Georgina breathed a sigh of relief when he had gone. She felt a little nervous when reciting messages on to the tape, but decided that for him to know of her nervousness, which he definitely would if she wrote the message down in longhand and left them on his desk, wasn't to be thought of. When she answered the phone to a sultry feminine voice who, on learning Tallis wasn't there, first of all said there was no message, then changed her mind, Georgina taped word for word what his caller had said. 'Naomi Garrick rang,' she recorded, 'she said "Thank you *so much* for a *perfectly heavenly evening*, and could you ring her".' Georgina had forgone the sultry note, but thought she had managed the correct intonation very well.

Tallis was sitting at his desk when she returned from lunch, the door between the two offices open. She knew that by now he would have played back the messages she had recorded, but since he didn't mention them, she didn't either.

When five o'clock came round she was so engrossed in her work, which, much as she had enjoyed the work she had done for Mr Parton, she found far more stimulating, that she was mindless of the time until she heard Tallis leave his desk. She looked up to see him standing in front of her.

'Working overtime?' he enquired, causing her to look at her watch.

'Ten past five!' she exclaimed, adding, 'Where has the afternoon gone to?'

'Enjoying your work?'

'I must do,' she replied, thinking that must be the case since the afternoon had flown by without her even noticing it. Then since he had a fine line in sarcasm, and she expected her reply to be met with some sarcastic observation, she looked up and saw he was looking down at her with an expression that looked friendly, as though it pleased him that she didn't find the work boring.

'You'd better get off home now,' he told her, his voice sounding as friendly as his look. 'You've put in a hard day today,' he tacked on, which inordinately pleased her. She recalled him saying Mr Parton had found no fault with her work—did it mean Tallis York could find no fault with her work either? She hoped so, for all she was unused to work at this level.

'I'll just finish this,' she said, not liking to leave anything in her typewriter overnight.

'Got a date tonight?' Tallis asked, before her fingers could go into action.

It was none of his business, of course, but since they seemed to be having their first fairly amicable conversation, she was reluctant to let fly and tell him so, or even lie and say yes, knowing he wouldn't blink at asking her if her date was with Desmond.

'No,' she answered, 'not tonight,' and waited expecting that even yet she might hear a sarcastic rejoinder even if there was no cause, but when had that ever stopped him?

She flicked a glance at him, and saw his look was still friendly, saw that he was smiling at her as though the fact that she wasn't seeing Desmond tonight pleased him. Well, it would, wouldn't it? she considered thoughtfully; he was now armed with the information, should Edgar Rankin require it, that his temporary secretary didn't see Edgar Rankin's son-in-law every evening.

'Does Mr Rankin know I'm working for you?' she asked, following her train of thought.

'Of course,' Tallis replied, the smile leaving him, causing her to think that some not very polite words had been exchanged between them on the subject.

'Oh,' she said quietly, then speaking without thought, 'Perhaps it would have been better to leave him in ignorance.'

She had said the wrong thing, she knew it as soon as she'd said it. Why had she said it anyway? she wondered as she saw any sign of being friendly had disappeared from his face. It didn't matter to her whether Edgar Rankin knew or not, she thought, and realised then that what lay behind her thinking was that if Tallis had left his uncle in ignorance, then he could have saved himself from some of his uncle's displeasure.

'When you get to know me better,' he said shortly, his expression cold, 'you'll know it's not my way to hide from my fellow board members or my family any decision I've made for which I might be criticised.' With that he left her, and she was pleased he did so, as she slammed into her typewriter. She went home without saying goodnight to him.

From now on, she decided furiously, her relationship

with him was going to be strictly business. If she was ever again mistaken enough to think she had seen a friendly light in his eyes for her then she would discount it utterly, and the next time he asked her if she had a date, she *would* tell him to mind his own business, and in no uncertain terms. And as for getting to know him better, there was going to be no chance of that—she knew as much of Tallis York as she want to know. I'll bet he doesn't get all nasty with Naomi Garrick, she thought, her pride badly bruised that Tallis York could put her in her place so cuttingly. No, he'd be sweetness and light with Naomi Garrick all the time, she thought mutinously. Well, he would, wouldn't he? From the sultry sound of her voice, not only did Naomi Garrick know the rules of the game, she had probably helped to invent them.

Tallis York was at the office before her the next morning. 'Good morning, Georgina,' he greeted her as she went in. No sign of animosity in his tones; perhaps he had been out with Naomi again last night and she had managed to sweeten him up, Georgina thought sourly.

'Good morning, Mr York,' she replied coolly, her armour of sophistication never more apparant than it was this morning.

'Drop your bag and come through,' he told her.

Georgina did as she was bidden, reflecting that it was going to be all go again today if he was ready to give dictation before she had taken her jacket off. She draped the grey jacket of her suit over the back of her chair, and not to be caught out again as she had been yesterday, picked up her notepad and pencil before going into the other room. Tallis looked up as she took the seat near his desk, her pencil poised. She saw his eyes flick over her, down the body-fitting outline of her white jersey shirt, before he turned his eyes back to her face.

'You can call me Tallis,' he invited, none of the coolness in him she had witnessed last night.

'Thank you,' said Georgina coolly. She wasn't going to yield an inch if he was all set to make friendly overtures this morning.

'Still mad with me?'

'Mad with you?' she queried in her best mystified manner, her tones remaining coolly polite. 'I'm sure I haven't any idea what ...'

She got no further, for as though he found his mirth impossible to contain, he burst out laughing, and her calm air of dignified composure threatened to desert her utterly as the sound of that very masculine amusement hit her ears, and she realised he was laughing at *her*!

'Oh, Georgina, you're priceless,' said Tallis, his laughter gone, but amusement still in his voice. 'I saw you were as mad as hell with me last night—not so much as a goodnight did I get, and you've come to work today all set to freeze me out, haven't you?'

'I've come here to work as your secretary. Other than you being the man I have to work for, I am not at all interested in personalities,' she said with rehearsed primness, hanging grimly on to every ounce of control as she saw the corners of his mouth threaten to curl up once more, as if he found her more than he could take.

'You don't think our working relationship might be more harmonious if we were a little—er—friendly?' he asked, and she was sure he was baiting her, since it couldn't bother him what their relationship was as long as the work got done.

'No, I don't,' she said firmly, watching as he sat back obviously expecting her to say more. But her composure had taken a jolt on being laughed at and she had no intention of prolonging this conversation, so she decided to get it all said and done with now. 'I thought you were being friendly last night,' she said with steady restraint, 'but the minute I let my guard down and let you see I was thinking only of the bother you could have saved yourself by not telling Edgar Rankin I'm working as your secretary —not that it matters to me either way,' she threw in off hand, 'you come down on me like a ton of bricks.'

'So you were mad,' he observed. 'I hurt your feelings, didn't I?'

'Since when has that ever bothered you?'

'I've hurt your feelings other times?' Georgina didn't answer. Any man who could hurl the accusations he had at her and think they hadn't hurt must be as insensitive as hell, was her considered opinion. 'I have, haven't I?' Tallis pressed. 'Would that be when I suggested you couldn't have been friends with Warner all that time without bed figuring in it somewhere?'

'It isn't important.'

That uncomfortable feeling was growing again that they were back to discussing that issue. Tallis was never going to believe her innocence anyway, so what was the point in going over old ground? Again she poised her pencil over her notepad, a broad hint if it was needed that she was taking no part in any discussion that wasn't to do with work.

'I think it is important,' she heard Tallis say, and there was no amusement in his voice now. In fact he sounded so deadly serious, it caused her to raise her head and look across at him. 'Have I gravely misjudged the situation, Georgina?' he asked her sincerely. 'Have I allowed the odd comment dropped here and there, together with what I know of life, of people, to cloud my judgment of one woman who might be different?'

She wanted to tell him she didn't care a damn about his

judgment, but she did. Oh, not because he was Tallis York, her boss, but simply because it had sickened her that any-one should believe what he had about her.

'I have no control over the conclusions you come to in your thinking,' she said, her voice quiet and nowhere as forceful as she would have liked. 'What I told you about Desmond Warner and myself was true. Whether you believe it or not is up to you.'

Tallis seemed arrested by the quietness of her tone, when before in defence her anger had been to the fore. He continued to look levelly at her for some moments, then he leaned forward and even before he spoke, maybe it was because there had been a hint on Tuesday that there was a doubt in his mind, but she had an idea that she had at last got through to him, and that he did believe her.

'*Honi soit qui mal y pense*,' he said at last. And then with a smile that would have thawed an iceberg, she thought, 'Are you going to forgive me for thinking the worst, Georgina?'

Why she should suddenly feel like crying, she had no idea. Relief, she supposed, relief that with all the odds stacked against her, Tallis York, with his knowledge of life, was giving her the benefit of the doubt, and not only that, but was asking her to forgive him. She forgot about being mad with him. Forgot all about how she had re-hearsed every step of the way to the office just exactly how she was going to be with him in future, how she was going to be cool and polite, but no more, and a smile that matched the warmth of the one he had given her broke from her.

'Yes,' she found herself saying. Then her smile froze as his look went to her mouth, to her eyes, and his own ex-pression became severe as if seeing her smile naturally at him had jolted him. Then she put it all down to her imagination that her smile had affected him in any way whatsoever, for the corners of his mouth were turning up again and he was saying:

'You're more generous than I deserve. Now let's get down to some work.'

It was funny, she thought, when she went out to lunch, how the morning had gone with such a swing after that. She had even called him Tallis at one point, she recalled, and she wouldn't have dreamt of doing that yesterday. But today was vastly different from yesterday, and though the work was much the same, the harmony in the air between them had certainly taken the strain out of the day.

He had to go out during the afternoon, and she was never more glad that this was the case when, answering the phone, she heard Desmond's voice saying he had rung Parton's and they had told him where to contact her, and would she go out with him that night.

Not knowing what time Tallis would be back, but strangely reluctant to want him to return while she was still speaking with Desmond, she began to feel hot and bothered. She still hadn't come to any final conclusion about Desmond, but knew their friendship was important to him. She couldn't bear to think of him being desperately lonely, but if ...

'Please say you'll come, Georgina,' Desmond pleaded, which was unlike him to plead.

'I ...' she hesitated, torn between her affection for him, and the remembrance of Tallis saying Lara would go back to him if she wasn't on the scene.

'I'll go round the bend if I have to sit in that apartment tonight!'

Georgina's hesitation lifted. She had heard Desmond when he had been low before, but she had never heard him as low as this. 'All right,' she capitulated fully, her heart aching for him that the joy she had witnessed when she had seen him with Lara had foundered. She felt it incumbent on her to try and lift him. 'We'll go somewhere madly gay, shall we?' she said, infusing a cheerful note into her voice, and heard relief in his voice that he wouldn't have only himself for company that evening, when she saw the handle of the outer door depress.

She felt the pink glow of colour wash her face, and didn't know why she should feel so guilty. She saw the door open a crack, heard Tallis's voice while at the same time taking note of the time Desmond had said he would call for her, and had said goodbye and replaced the phone to realise that Tallis had been buttonholed by someone in the corridor and was talking outside.

By the time he came in, Georgina's colour had returned to normal and she was busy at her typewriter.

'Any messages?' Tallis asked pleasantly, stopping by her desk on his way through.

'I wasn't sure when you'd be back, so I put them on the tape,' she told him. Naomi Garrick had phoned again today.

Georgina was in no hurry to get dressed ready to go out. Desmond had said he would call at eight. She hoped he would be in a mood where she could talk to him—what Tallis had said about Lara was worrying.

When at seven o'clock the outside door bell to her flat rang, she was still in the suit she had worn to work that day, and went down the flight of stairs to answer it.

'Desmond!' she exclaimed, her heart going out to him that he looked as though he hadn't had any sleep since the last time she had seen him. Though if he had been having sleepless nights on account of Lara, she thought it best not to refer to the tired look in his eyes. 'I didn't expect you until eight,' she said cheerfully, standing back to allow him to come in so she could close the door.

'I said I'd be here at seven,' said Desmond.

'Oh, did you? My mistake,' she answered, realising she had been so anxious to finish the call before Tallis came and caught her talking to Desmond, suspecting that once he knew the identity of her caller the growing harmony between them would be shattered; she must have misheard the time Desmond had said. 'Well, never mind,' she continued brightly. 'It won't take me long to get ready— you can come and read the paper while you're waiting,' she said, though in her view it would do him far more good if he closed his eyes and took a nap while he was waiting.

'How long is it going to take you to get ready?' he asked.

'Half an hour at the most,' she said.

'Would you mind very much if I brought my briefcase in and did some work—I still haven't caught up from my Belgium trip yet?'

'I'll make you a cup of coffee to drink while you're working,' Georgina told him, and waited at the front door while he returned to his car for his briefcase.

CHAPTER FIVE

In the end they didn't go anywhere madly gay. Georgina could see Desmond looked too weary to want to make the effort to be the life and soul of the party, and she fell in easily with his suggestion that they dine at a quiet restaurant they had been to before.

Wanting to know how he had got on with Lara the other night, though being far too sensitive to bring the subject up until he did since it was blatantly obvious that the happiness she and Tallis had witnessed in them must have curdled, Georgina spoke lightly of her being seconded to fill the breach for Tallis's permanent secretary.

'You get on all right with him?' Desmond asked, and she could see he was making an effort to lift himself out of his despondency.

'Oh yes,' she answered. Well, she had today, she thought, and stifled the urge to tell him of the vile rumours that were circulating in his wife's family about the depth of their friendship. He seemed to have enough on his plate, and anyway since Tallis had revised his previous opinion it no longer seemed that important, though she wasn't quite sure why Tallis York's good opinion of her should matter all that much. Natural distaste, she thought, for something that wasn't quite nice. Then, dismissing all thoughts of what had gone on previously between her and Tallis, she chatted to Desmond about the high-speed outfit she now found herself part of, and what a demon Tallis was for work.

'It was a surprise to learn that you and Tallis knew each other,' said Desmond suddenly, his first reference to the night the four of them had dined together.

'It was a surprise to me too,' Georgina said carefully—the last thing she wanted to do was to bring Lara up if he wasn't yet ready to talk about her—'to find you're indirectly related to him.'

'Didn't I ever mention—that Lara's family had connections with Chestertons?' he asked, an expression crossing his face that was painful to watch as he brought out his wife's name. Then answering his own question, he went on bitterly, 'No, I don't suppose I did, since Chestertons is at the root of why Lara left me.' His bitterness then changed to anguish. 'God, I wish I'd never heard of the damned company—if it wasn't for Lara's high-falutin' ideas of seeing me on their board, she might still be living with me now.'

Georgina accepted what he said about Chestertons being at the root of his marital problems, but she remembered he had also told her his marriage had been squally before that particular dispute had come up. And if Lara loved him as Tallis said, then she didn't think much of her for putting prestige before that love. Granted, both Desmond and Lara were being strong-minded over this issue, but to let it drag on for twelve months without either of them giving in spoke of a peculiar sort of love to her. Yet what did she know of love? She'd been at pains to avoid any but the lightest of involvement with the opposite sex.

Sensing since Desmond had been the one to mention Lara's name that he might want to talk about Monday night, Georgina sought in her mind for something to say that would give him an opening he could either take up or leave.

'You didn't mind Tallis taking me home the other night, did you?' she asked, referring to the fact that he had been left alone with Lara, though if he didn't take her meaning, he could well think she was apologising because it wasn't the done thing to go somewhere with one man and come home with another.

'Not at all,' he said, and she could have wished Edgar Rankin had heard him, because it was crystal clear to her and would have been to anyone else listening that Desmond looked on her as a friend and nothing more. 'I was glad of the opportunity to be alone with Lara, actually,' he confessed bleakly, 'so you taking those papers home that Tallis wanted seemed most fortuitous from my point of view.' Briefly Desmond lost his look of hopelessness as he remembered, 'That was a wonderful evening for me. I had the Belgian contract signed and sealed. And though I'll admit the evening started off badly as far as I was concerned, when you and Tallis went to dance, Lara suddenly dropped the cold shoulder treatment and became the woman I married. It was marvellous, Georgina,' he said, and his eyes actually shone. 'After you left, Lara and I danced and I felt twenty years old again, and I'm sure she felt the same.'

His eyes looked past her as he went away from her recalling the way it had been, and Georgina had to swallow down tears on seeing that look on his face, knowing that despair would be his when he came down to earth again. Didn't Lara know what she was doing to him? She was tearing him apart.

'It didn't end there,' he went on. 'After we left the Bellington, Lara said she'd like to see inside the apartment again. I couldn't believe she meant it because she hadn't been anywhere near since the day she packed her bags and left.

Desmond stopped speaking for a while, his expression telling her she had no part in his private thoughts, and she felt choked that at some point everything must have gone tragically wrong to have sent him down into the depths he had been in earlier. Then he blinked, the light faded from his eyes and all the misery and unhappiness flooded in. She saw his hand clench on the table, wanted to place her hand over his in compassion, but didn't because she was fond enough of him to know she would cry if he gripped on to her hand like some drowning man. She saw he too had to swallow, but he was in control when he told her tonelessly:

'What fools love makes of us—I was living in a fantasy world thinking Lara would leave her father and come back to me the next day.' He laughed a laugh that had no pleasure in it, and showed a cynicism that Georgina had not seen in him before. 'We were having breakfast,' he told her, 'when Lara told me the seat on the board at Chestertons could still be mine if I wanted it, that her father was considering retiring and a way would be open for me to get in,' he paused and sighed deeply. 'Before I knew what was happening, we were in the middle of a blazing row, and I knew then that Lara was holding out for the same conditions.'

Georgina was surprised that Lara had stayed the night with him, for that was what must have happened since he had spoken of their having breakfast together. But she was more surprised that even after giving of herself Lara was still holding out for going back on her terms. No wonder Desmond was so desolate! He must have thought the bone of contention between them had been buried, only to find it was still there for them both to gnaw at.

She didn't give credence any more to what Tallis had said about her blocking the way of Lara going back to Desmond, and in the face of his heart-sickness, she didn't see anyway how she could think of discontinuing their friendship. Then she remembered that venomous look Lara had given her, and her whole thinking turned upside down making her wonder if there was something in what Tallis had said after all. She just had to find out.

'Desmond,' she said, and stopped, not sure how to go on. 'Er—you don't think Lara is—upset because you're friendly with me, do you?'

'Friendly with you?' he echoed, obviously not with her, then catching on, 'Jealous, do you mean?' He gave a bitter laugh. 'Not Lara. She knows she had no cause to be jealous —she knows there's no other woman for me but her.'

'So you don't think that Lara might ...' Georgina stopped, not liking Tallis York very much that because of what he had said she was now stumbling her way through something that would never have occurred to either her or Desmond. 'What I mean is, if I was out of the way do you think it would be one obstacle less in the way of you and Lara getting back together again?'

'I've just told you the only obstacle in the way,' Desmond said. 'I'm just not going to work for Chestertons. My own business is starting to pick up, this Belgian contract has given it a tremendous boost, and ...' he broke off suddenly, his expression wretched. 'Oh, for God's sake, Georgina, don't you desert me now,' he said hoarsely, his hand coming across the table to grip her with fierce intensity. 'Seeing you, knowing I can come and talk to you, is my safety valve I suppose,' he confessed. 'You're the only thing that keeps me and sanity hanging together. Don't, please Georgina, don't take your friendship away from me now.'

Hurriedly she rushed in to reassure him, and by the time their meal had finished and he took her home, she thought she had convinced him that she didn't want to break their friendship.

But once inside her flat she went straight to bed. Never had she felt so drained, so exhausted. What had started out as a friendship with Desmond because he was lonely, and had continued because he was a safe escort, and had grown from there into a brother-and-sister type of relationship, now threatened to be wearing on her reserves of strength. She now felt as down as Desmond had been, as though in trying to lift his depression she had taken it from him and on to herself. She lay in bed trying to remember that Desmond wasn't always like this, that given a week or two he would begin to pull out of it.

The ringing of the door bell brought her up out of the

depths of sleep. Turning her head, she looked at the clock, and thought it providential that someone was ringing at her door bell, for she had forgotten to set her alarm, and it was now half past seven.

Diving for her dressing gown, she shrugged into it, tying up the belt as she pattered down the stairs. She brushed her hair back from her face as she pulled open the front door.

'Desmond!' she exclaimed on seeing him there. 'What ...?'

'Sorry to call so early,' he apologised, then explained, 'I forgot to take my briefcase when we went out last night.'

'Oh,' said Georgina, thinking he looked much better this morning, as though he'd had a good night's sleep. 'Come on up. Where did you leave it?' she asked as he went with her up the stairs. 'I didn't notice it.'

'Down by the side of the settee,' he told her, and as they entered her sitting room, 'There it is—I'd be lost without it.' Then as if he had only just noticed she hadn't had time to get dressed, he apologised again for disturbing her, adding, 'I'll see myself out.'

'I'd better come and close the front door after you,' she said. 'You know how the whole house shakes if it isn't closed from the outside with a key.' She clearly remembered the way her windows had rattled when Tallis had pulled it to after him on Monday, and was mindful of any of her fellow apartment-dwellers who might still be asleep.

She went down the stairs with Desmond, with him talking in quiet tones in case they disturbed her neighbours, asking her what she was doing at the weekend, and standing for a few moments at the open front door to tell her he'd give her a ring next week, telling her he had decided to go away for the weekend himself. Georgina thought it might do him good to get away for a few days and smiled at him as he went on to explain that a friend of his had just bought some property with a stretch of river belonging to it.

He was still talking when her eyes went past him to see a car that looked vaguely familiar, slow down as it drew nearer. And then as she recognised the driver, Georgina just didn't hear a word Desmond was saying. Her heart turned a near somersault as the car drew level, she saw Tallis York look at her, his expression filled with contempt, before he put his foot down and travelled on. And she had no trouble at all in telling from that contemptuous look exactly what he was thinking.

No, no, it's not what you think, she wanted to run after him and cry. But he was already turning the corner and going out of her line of vision, and Desmond was telling her:

'. . . so I thought with the trout fishing season just around the corner I'd take up his invitation and have a look at his stretch of river,' adding, 'Well, I must be off or I'll lose the benefit of my early start.'

Back in her flat Georgina caught sight of herself in the mirror—hair all tousled, dressing gown hastily pulled on. Oh God, she groaned, recalling Tallis's contemptuous look. Yesterday he had believed her about being friends only with Desmond, today a pneumatic drill wouldn't get through his set opinion on what he had seen. It passed through her mind to enlist Desmond's help. If she got Desmond to ring Tallis and explain . . . She discounted the idea. Desmond hadn't even seen him go by, besides which Desmond had looked to be on the edge of cracking up last night. True, he had looked so much better this morning, but that wasn't to say the burden of his thoughts wouldn't get him down as the day went on. No, she thought, he had enough to cope with, and anyway—pride rearing its head—what did it matter to her what Tallis York believed?

She went and had her bath prior to getting dressed ready to go to work, somehow she had a feeling that the harmony that had been between her and Tallis York yesterday wouldn't be anywhere in evidence today.

She was right about that. No sooner had she set foot inside her office door than she knew the harmony of yesterday was a thing of the past. The door between the two offices stood open and she saw Tallis at his desk as though waiting for her to come in. He didn't smile, didn't even look to be aware she was there, and if she was waiting for him to call, 'Good morning, Georgina', as he had done yesterday, then she could tell it would be better for her not to hold her breath as she waited; she'd expire first.

On impulse she moved towards his door, 'Tallis . . .' she began, but the glowering look he gave her stopped her.

'I've put your dictation on tape,' he told her, his voice sounding brick-hard, letting her know she'd be wasting her time trying to get through. 'Close the door on your way out,' he dismissed her.

Georgina went out, closing the door with a sharp snap. Who did he think he was to set himself up as the judge of her morals? Anger mingled with a feeling of being aggrieved that he could yesterday have been prepared to listen to her, but that today he couldn't even bear to have her in the same office as himself to give her dictation. And to dismiss her like that, as if she was of no account! Pride stormed in to be added to her other feelings, and taking the cover off her typewriter, she determined that never, ever again would she discuss with him anything that wasn't connected with business. To hell with him! she thought, riding high on outrage. She didn't give a damn what he thought of her anyway. Sparks fairly flew out of her type-writer as she hammered out some of her fury.

She had been working solidly for an hour when the door opened and Tallis came through. She refused to look at him, refused to stop work, had a feeling he was standing watching her, but concentrated on what she was doing, not wanting to make a mistake and have to stop and correct it, thereby letting him know he was unnerving her. Of course she did make a mistake, but, too stubborn to let him know he had penetrated her concentration and was the cause of her making the error, she dropped her hands away from the keys and looked up.

She met coal-black eyes, that were as hard, and his ex-pression about the same, full on. 'Can I do something for you?' she asked coolly, thinking he must have been waiting for her to stop before he told her what he wanted.

He continued to survey her in grim silence, then the look on his face changed to one of disparagement, his very tone insulting. 'You do something for me?' he enquired. 'Not a thing.' He waited only to see from the angry glint in her eyes that she had got his meaning, then he turned to the other door and strolled out.

Georgina seethed quietly after he had gone. Oh, to be in a position not to be here when he came back! Oh, to be able to leave him a sweetly voiced message on tape telling him exactly what he could do with this job. She'd have to be thick not to have gathered what he meant by 'Not a thing', she fumed. She'd been referring to business, but he had promptly, with his warped mind, put a personal conno-tation on her question, and the insolence of his tone left her in no doubt that he thought Desmond wanted his head looked at, for fancying anything she had to offer.

The phone rang just as he came back through the door some ten minutes later. Georgina left her typing to answer it. 'Hello, Georgina, Lara Warner here,' said a bright voice. 'It Tallis free, by any chance?'

'I'll put you through,' Georgina told her, not bothering to wait to ask Tallis if he would take the call. 'Mrs Warner for you,' she said, determined to keep all her dealings with him formal when she could just as easily have said, 'Lara for you.'

'I'll take it in my office,' he grunted.

Georgina wasn't in the least bit interested in Tallis's end of the conversation, and wished he had remembered to close the door behind him. Just seeing the dark suit of him, the shape of him, the dark arrogant head as he stood with his back to her, had her renewing her anger against him. And then her anger fled, for from what she could make out from his replies, Lara had changed rapidly from the bright and alive person who had asked to speak with him, and now, from what she could gather, seemed to be most upset. The next thing Tallis said confirmed this suspicion.

'Don't cry, Lara,' she heard him say. 'He isn't worth your tears.' There was a pause, then, his voice hardening, 'He told you that?' There was another pause and Georgina made no pretence of working, barely conscious that she was listening in, she heard Tallis say, 'Regardless of that fact, I'm sure it won't last.' At that point Tallis swung round, caught Georgina's eyes on him, then holding her eyes, some magnet in his severe dark look making her unable to tear her eyes away, he told Lara, 'She may be beautiful to look at, but in my view she hasn't got very much else to recommend her—he'll get tired of her before very long, I feel sure. Take my word for it, she won't be his mistress for very much longer.'

Georgina's eyes widened as she stared back at him. They were talking about her, there was no mistaking it! A fiery red came up under her skin, and without thinking about it she was on her feet just as Tallis favoured her with another of his insolent looks and casually turned his back on her. She heard him tell Lara to dry her eyes and that he would take her out to lunch, and waited no longer than it took him to replace the phone when she went storming into his office.

'How dare you speak of me like that!' she raged even before he had turned round.

He did so then, and if he had noted that she looked magnificent in her fury, there was nothing in his face to tell her of it as he surveyed her outraged face coolly.

'Which part did you object to?' he drawled insolently. 'I'm sure you've heard yourself described as beautiful before.'

'It wasn't that part, and you damn well know it,' she raged, uncaring that he knew she had been listening, and further outraged that he thought her so low, he didn't care that she had been listening anyhow.

'You're piqued because I told Lara her husband will soon tire of you?' he enquired, letting her know that her being 'piqued' had no effect on him whatsoever, when in Georgina's view she felt more apoplectic than 'piqued'. 'Or are you peeved because I said you haven't much other than your beauty with which to hold a man?'

That stung, she rather thought it was meant to, but she was too worked up to think then why Tallis York's opinion of her and her inability to hold a man should hurt.

'Your opinion of me doesn't bother me in the slightest,' she flamed, and disregarded that his eyes had narrowed at that. 'Though only yesterday you were believing what I told you about the true situation between Desmond and me, but now here you are telling *his wife* that I'm his mistress! You ...'

'Which just shows how wrong I can be,' he cut in

harshly. 'Yesterday I thought I saw an honesty in you that had me going against my better judgment. This morning I saw Warner leaving your apartment with you looking as though you'd only just tumbled out of your mutual bed to see him off. No,' he held up a hand as she would have hotly interrupted him 'I'm sick to the back teeth of your lies, your dishonesty. Despite what Warner told Lara, you haven't even the guts to be open about the way things are between the two of you.'

'Despite what ...' Georgina began, her fury being tempered by confusion. What could Desmond tell Lara about their relationship that wouldn't do anything but confirm the innocence of it?

'Lara was speaking with him a few minutes before she rang me,' she was informed coldly. 'She's just been breaking her heart because of what her husband told her—she thinks she doesn't stand a chance of being reconciled with him now.'

Georgina's fury died as she tried to see what Lara's angle was. Lara knew perfectly well that Desmond wanted her back, but she knew she would be wasting her time arguing that point with Tallis. He wasn't ready any longer to believe a word she said. But what in heaven's name had Desmond told her that should send her crying to Tallis?

'Lara was upset after speaking with Desmond?' she queried, wanting to know why, since it appeared she was at the centre of Lara's distress.

'A perfectly natural feeling for any woman in the position she's in, I would have thought,' Tallis answered coldly, a look of distaste crossing his face. 'She's well aware of the situation between you and Warner, there was no need for him to rub it in by telling her that you're in love with him.'

'In love with him?' Georgina echoed, startled. 'Desmond told her that?'

'Do you deny that it's true?'

Had his tone been warmer, had there been any hint anywhere about him that her denial might have been believed, she might well have made the effort to again clear herself in his eyes. But she had never seen any virtue in banging her head against a brick wall, and with Tallis looking so iron-hard, she wasn't going to try it. It was because she was trying to make head or tail of what was going on; had Desmond really said that? Was Lara making it up for some devious reason of her own? It had her saying:

'Would you believe me if I did?'

She saw her answer in the ever hard, unbending line of him, and without waiting to hear his reply, she turned and left him.

When Tallis walked by her desk just before lunch, she kept her head buried deep in her work, and only when the door had closed after him did she lift her head. He was having lunch with Lara, and it didn't take two guesses to know that Georgina Underwood's name wouldn't come out from that lunch any greyer than it was already.

She came back from her own lunch firmly decided that when Tallis went to a meeting he had scheduled for three o'clock, then she was definitely going to ring Desmond to find out what was going on. Whether he was in a mood to hear Lara's name mentioned or not, she just had to find out what was happening. Had he really told Lara that she was in love with him, or, as her earlier suspicion grew, was it Lara who had made that up for her own ends?

It was nearly four before Georgina was free to make her call to Desmond. As had happened on previous occasions, the minute Tallis was out of the office, the phone seemed to have rung continuously. Her voice crisp, she had faithfully recorded all his messages. But when she did get through to Desmond's office, it was only to be informed by his secretary that he had already left.

'Not to worry,' she told Anne Scrivener, 'I'll probably be able to contact him at home.'

'He wasn't returning home,' Anne, who had spoken to Georgina often before, told her. 'He's going away for the weekend and left early to avoid being caught up in traffic.'

I'm fed up, Georgina thought when she came off the phone. Completely and utterly fed up. Secretary, if only temporary—hurry back, Mrs Fry—to a flint-faced man who had been hard pressed to spare her one word when he'd returned from lunch—thank you, Lara, she thought, with a cynicism that had never been part of her nature. She was in the middle, by the look of it, of a marital wrangle that seemed no nearer to being resolved. Too scared to do what every right-thinking bone in her body told her would be the best action and stop seeing Desmond, because she was oh, so dreadfully afraid he would crack up if she withdrew her friendship at this point. Everybody around her seemed to be going about with long faces, she thought. Her own couldn't be called an exception, because she hadn't exactly shone today either, had she? She thought of her home in Kenilworth, of Maggie with her never-failing good humour, and suddenly her mind was made up. She would go to Kenilworth this weekend, and blow the lot of them.

She was sitting in the train heading for Coventry that night, Kenilworth station having been axed long since, and already she was beginning to feel better. She hadn't seen Tallis York again since he had gone to his meeting, and she was glad about that. Monday morning and *him* would come round too soon for her liking!

But at Kenilworth something happened that had Georgina going back to London with something else to think about. There had been no one in when she had tried to phone before leaving London, but she had got through to Maggie before catching the bus in Coventry, and saw Nicola come racing down the road to meet her as soon as she turned the corner into the road where they lived. Chattering ten to the dozen, Nicola insisted on carrying her weekend case the short distance to the house.

'How's school?' Georgina asked, espying Josh standing by the gate. He took his role of man of the house very seriously, and for all Georgina knew herself loved by him, he was less exuberant than his sister when it came to showing emotion. Georgina waved to him and he waved back, opening the gate as he did so.

'Don't mention school,' said a resigned Nicola by her side. 'I'm trying to forget about it until Monday. Roll on, school holidays!' Georgina laughed down at her. Nicola with her rebellious spirit claimed she had hated school since her very first day. 'Another two years of purgatory to look forward to!' Nicola groaned comically, and then they were up to Josh.

Because she was so very fond of him, it took Georgina all her time not to put her arms around him and give him the same hug she had given Nicola. But she was aware that Josh was going through a stage in his development when such a demonstration, which might be witnessed by neighbours, would mightily embarrass him, so she settled for planting the briefest of kisses on his cheek, but he knew her affection was there for him when she said a quiet, 'Hello, love.'

Josh relieved Nicola of Georgina's case, his usually serious face for once smiling, as he asked had she had a good journey. How grown up he was sounding, Georgina thought, as she replied and smiled at him in return. He'd had to grow up quickly, she thought, for all Maggie didn't take her responsibilities lightly. It was Josh himself who had taken it on himself to do what he considered to be the man's jobs around the house.

Then Josh opened the back door, and there was Maggie. Dear, wonderful Maggie, her figure slightly rounded, her brown hair sprinkled with grey, but those hazel eyes shining with love and welcome for her stepdaughter. No words were spoken. Maggie just opened her arms and folded Georgina to her, and Georgina was happy, London and all thoughts of her ghastly day faded. It was good to be home.

It irritated Georgina that unwanted thoughts of Tallis York should penetrate her mind at odd moments over the weekend. Having thought like Nicola that she could forget about all things unpleasant until Monday, she found it particularly annoying that he should fill her thoughts that Friday night as she lay sleepless in her bed. More annoying still was the fact that however hard she tried to dislodge him from her thoughts, tried to think of something else, he just refused to be dislodged.

On Saturday she helped with the usual Saturday morning chores, then in the afternoon the four of them took a walk over the Abbey Fields. It had been in her mind to tell Maggie something of her worries over continuing her friendship with Desmond, but when Maggie asked, Josh and Nicola having walked on some way in front, 'How's Desmond?' Georgina found she just couldn't confide in her. It all sounded, oh—so sordid somehow, and though Maggie was no prude, it just didn't seem right to bring what seemed to her then dirty washing home.

'He's fine,' she replied, perhaps not as quickly as she might have done, she realised, for Maggie was quick to ask:

'You still see him?'

'Oh yes. He's been away on business, as I wrote and told

you, but he's back now. I had dinner with him twice this week.'

'You do have other escorts besides him, though?'

Because she was so very fond of Maggie, Georgina's ears picked up a note in her voice that seemed to make her question sound more important than it should. 'Sometimes,' she answered truthfully, remembering she always mentioned who she went out with when writing home, and a little puzzled at the question. Then, wondering if that note in Maggie's voice meant she was as disapproving of her going out with Desmond as everyone else seemed to be, she hastened to tell her, 'Desmond and I are only friends, Maggie, nothing more.'

How wonderful it was to have someone believe in her! The look that Maggie straightaway gave her told her she had never considered her friendship with him to be anything else. It was good to hear her laugh and call her a dope, and to know Maggie had never meant any such thing.

'I know that,' said Maggie stoutly, her laughter fading. 'Desmond would need a friend like you if that wife of his is still giving him the runaround. Any signs of them getting back together again?'

'Not much,' said Georgina carefully, 'and the months keep ticking by.'

'Well, they'll sort themselves out when they're ready, I expect,' commented Maggie, and they went on to talk of other things.

But it was the following day, after a lunch where much laughter had presided, and Georgina had decided she would put off returning to London and catch an early train back in the morning, as she and Maggie sat, each ensconced in an easy chair, on either side of a roaring fire, that the conversation took a turn Georgina found disquieting. Nicola was out somewhere with a couple of her friends who had come to call, and Josh was outside the kitchen door overhauling the bike Nicola had complained about more than once in the last two days because the chain kept coming off.

Maggie's face was for once deadly serious as she returned to the question she had asked yesterday—did Georgina go out with anyone other than Desmond. And again that tone was in her voice that Georgina had misread yesterday, and suddenly Georgina's pangs of disquiet were growing into pangs of alarm; for it looked as though Maggie had been doing some very deep thinking and had come up with some answers that were much too close for comfort.

'Your letters home are always newsy,' she continued, 'and we all rush to read them. But when I write back and ask how Hugh or Ian is,' she mentioned two of her step-daughter's most recent escorts, 'in your return letters, you always say you're no longer going out with them. You've lived in London a long time,' she went on, still in that same serious way that was rare coming from Maggie, 'and I know from the time you lived at home that you never had any trouble keeping boy-friends, so I don't think it can be you that's at fault that you never seem to go out with the same man, other than Desmond, more than a couple of times.'

Georgina's alarm grew. She hadn't given a thought, in her plans to stay single, to the fact that Maggie would read so much into the letters she had written home. What a shortsighted idiot she had been! But before she could make some lighthearted comment to the effect that Maggie was biased in her favour, Maggie was going on:

'And I can't think, Desmond apart, that not one of the men you've been out with since your father died didn't have something in him that wouldn't have you wanting to know him better.'

Her father had been dead five years, and those words, 'since your father died' told Georgina more clearly than anything that Maggie's thoughts had hit the target dead centre.

'Maggie . . .' she began, only to have Maggie saying:

'No, let me finish. It's been on my mind for some time. You're far too loyal to us, Georgina, and we love you for it, but I can't help worrying about you.'

'Worrying about me!' That was the last thing she wanted. 'Maggie, there's no need. Honestly . . .'

'I think there's every need,' Maggie interrupted her. 'I know you, Georgina—know you and am grateful for your loyalty to us. But that doesn't stop me from wondering if because of that loyalty you're missing out on life. It doesn't stop me from wondering if we take too much from you.' Again Georgina made to hurriedly say something, but Maggie shook her head, 'I have to say this, it's been in my mind for a long time,' she repeated, when Georgina wanted to stop her, and Maggie went solemnly on. 'You'll be twenty-six next week. I know you, remember well all the soul-searching I helped you with when that independent streak of yours urged you to go to London the year before your father died. But for all your independent streak, basically you're a home-maker. You love family life, and I can't help but worry that the reason you haven't married yet is because you're putting us first.'

'Oh, Maggie,' Georgina cried, unable to stay quiet, appalled that Maggie must have been worrying for some time to have reached this conclusion but had never said anything, 'I'm single because the right man hasn't asked me to marry him yet.'

'But would you accept him if he did?' Maggie questioned. 'Would you allow yourself to fall in love?' She paused momentarily. 'Or, knowing something of that emotion, if you fell in love, would you welcome it, allow your heart to rule your head? Or would you, as I suspect, turn your back on love out of some misguided feeling that we need the money you send every month too badly for you to give up your job to take on the role of wife and have babies?'

'Of course I would,' Georgina lied promptly. Too promptly, she saw immediately, for Maggie shook her head.

'Oh, Georgie,' she sighed, using the family pet abbreviation for her name. 'You're such a dear girl, but I don't think you're being very truthful. You've made up your mind not to marry until Josh has his place at university—and probably not then, probably not until he can write M.B. after his name.' Maggie's face, normally cheerful against all odds, suddenly looked so woebegone that instantly Georgina was out of her chair and going to her.

'Don't be unhappy, Maggie, please,' she begged—and spent the next half an hour trying to impress on her that she wasn't missing out on one solitary thing and that it was as she had said it was, the right man hadn't asked her to marry him yet, but that when he did she would accept him without hesitation. Just why she should think of Tallis York just then she had no idea. She promptly ejected him from her mind, and put all her efforts into trying to get that look off Maggie's face.

Georgina went to bed that night with her mind heavy with worry. She had managed, she thought, to persuade Maggie she wasn't making sacrifices for the children, but she couldn't stop being anxious when she wondered for just how long Maggie had been nursing these worries.

CHAPTER SIX

THE following morning Georgina sat in the train heading for London knowing she was going to be an hour late arriving at the office. She had been up early enough, they all had, or so they thought, but the sudden discovery, by courtesy of the radio, that British Summer Time had begun had them all chasing around.

Nicola was ready to dash out of the house without breakfast in panic at knowing she was going to receive another black mark for being late, as the radio announcer taunted, 'You did remember to put your clocks forward, didn't you?' While Josh, who had been very quiet—he'd been quiet last night too, she recalled, as though he had something on his mind—forgot whatever it was that was bothering him, and because he played chess every Monday after school, went searching for his 'lucky' chess men Nicola had put 'somewhere'. It had been Maggie who had helped them to see the funny side of it when Georgina, about to join in the scramble, was all set to charge upstairs to put her last minute things inside her case.

Remembering the way Tallis had been with her on Friday, Georgina didn't think he was going to think it funny. Then she decided not to think about him at all until she had to—no point in anticipating trouble—and the rest of the train journey was taken up with thoughts of the weekend, of thinking of the conversation she had had with Maggie yesterday, remembering the presents they had given her for her birthday next week that Maggie had already parcelled up ready for the post on Saturday.

Georgina had been instructed by all three of them not to
open it until Wednesday. She recalled telling them about
her working for Chestertons now, and sensing that Maggie
had noticed her reticence when Tallis York's name cropped
up, she had suspected she might be giving Magie something else to worry about, so she had told her he was a
charming man and that she liked him very much. Hoping
to be forgiven for her sins, she had quickly changed the
subject.

Once the train stopped at Euston she had no time to give
her thoughts free rein: all her energies centred on getting
to the office in the quickest possible time. When the taxi
dropped her off, she checked the hands of her watch, put
ahead an hour that morning, and saw it was nearly ten
o'clock.

She was all ready with her explanation for being late
when she opened the office door, but seeing Tallis York
come from his office, his expression more arctic than arctic
as he looked from her to the weekend case in her hand, she
knew before she so much as opened her mouth that anything she had to say was not going to be believed. He
looked madder than hell. She opened her mouth to try
anyway, her heart bumping chaotically, but got no further
than, 'I'm ...' before he was slamming into her with his
aggression thundering down on her head.

'You don't give a damn, do you,' he barked, coming to
stand barely inches away from her. 'You don't give a damn
who gets hurt so long as you have your enjoyment!'

'I'm sorry I'm late,' Georgina tried quickly when it
looked as though his temper was going to go out of control,
and hoping her apology might ease the situation. All this
because she was an hour late? And what was he talking
about anyway? Who was she hurting? 'I've been away for
the weekend, and ...'

'I know damn well where you've been, and with whom!'

he thundered, making her take a rapid pace away from him when it looked as though he was going to take hold of her and shake the living daylights out of her.

'Y-you know ...?' she said, her bewilderment growing. She hadn't said a word to him about going to Kenilworth. In fact she'd only made up her mind to go after he had gone to his meeting on Friday. And who was she supposed to have gone with ...?

'Did you think to keep it a secret? Not that you'd care. It wouldn't enter your pleasure-seeking little mind to stop and consider the hurt you're causing someone else. You've gone so far with your affair with Warner it just doesn't matter to you in your adulterous association with him that his wife is breaking her heart!'

'Adulterous association!' Georgina exclaimed, her fear of him dying as her temper rose. 'Now stop right th ...' she started to flare, only to find Tallis had no intention of stopping anywhere, for his voice was raised over the top of hers.

'You thought no one would find out, didn't you? Not that it would have bothered you. But Warner wouldn't want his wife to know. Regardless of what you think you have going for you, he still cares enough for her to want to keep his movements secret from her.' At that point, as though his fury was too much to contain, he did take hold of her. She felt his hard hands biting uncaringly into her upper arms. 'A pity for you,' he snarled, 'that Lara rang Warner's office late on Friday ready to apologise for any harsh things she might have said when she spoke to him that morning. His secretary didn't hesitate to tell her he'd gone away for the weekend.'

In that instant Georgina knew she didn't even want to try and clear herself. Let them all get on with it. Let them all stew and draw their own mucky conclusions! If Lara spent less time thinking about herself and more about the husband she was now professing to care for, she would see he was heading for a breakdown before too long.

'And what else did *dear* Lara have to tell you?' she asked, with a brave attempt at sarcasm, hoping her face wasn't showing her fear when the grip on her arms tightened and Tallis gave a sharply indrawn breath thinking that she didn't seem to care who got hurt providing it wasn't her. Then as though aware the violence of his temper might get out of hand, he let go his hold on her and rammed his hands in his trouser pockets, and the next time he spoke the heat in him was controlled, his voice icy.

'My cousin has joined forces with my uncle in recommending that the likes of you are of no great asset to this company,' he told her through tight lips. 'I'm inclined to agree with them.'

Georgina kept her features outwardly calm, though she felt herself grow pale. 'So I'm to be dismissed after all,' she said tonelessly.

'Oh no, Miss Underwood, that would be too easy,' said Tallis. 'I've given you my word your job is safe, and though I'm fully aware the word "honour" doesn't appear in your personal dictionary, I have no intention of breaking my word.' He took a step away, deliberately letting his eyes scan over her face and figure, making no hurry to return his eyes to her face, but when he did, there was a granite-hard look in his eyes as he promised. 'No, Miss Underwood, I'm not going to dismiss you, but make no mistake about it, I shall find some way of sorting you out.' Then with all the calm assurance of a man who always had the upper hand, he just turned his back on her and left the office.

Georgina's thoughts were in uproar after he had gone.

Such flaming fury! Such ice-cold calm! She felt as though she'd been chewed, eaten up, and spat out again, and was glad to sink on to her chair, needing something solid beneath her while she went over everything that had happened.

Automatically, it seemed, she coped with her work that day, hanging on grimly to the only redeeming feature of Tallis York's indictment of her. He had promised she wouldn't be losing her job, and nothing was going to make him break his word. She had to hang on to that, though that wouldn't stop her from looking round for something else meantime. How could she continue to work for a man who not only had no opinion at all of her, but had clearly stated that somehow or other, he was going to 'sort her out'?

When Desmond rang half way through the afternoon, she was in no mood to want to speak to him. Then the thoughts she'd had about him heading for a breakdown returned, and it just wasn't in her to turn her back on him. Though he must have picked up from her voice that something was bothering her, for he asked:

'Is anything the matter?'

About to say no, Georgina found herself asking, 'Er— Desmond—Did you tell Lara I was in love with you?' She wished she hadn't asked it as soon as the question had left her, for she was sure now that Lara had made that up, the same way she had paired her off with him over the weekend. But in the lengthening pause that followed, her certainty began to waver. 'Desmond?' she prompted.

'Well, actually . . .' he said slowly.

'Oh, Desmond, you didn't!' she said disbelievingly.

'I'm sorry,' he hastened to apologise. 'I didn't mean to, believe me, but . . .'

'But you *know* it *isn't* true,' Georgina exclaimed. 'You

know I'm fond of you, but I have never ever given you to understand...'

'I know, I know,' he said quickly, 'and I wouldn't have said what I did if Lara hadn't goaded me into it. She was being a bit spiteful actually,' he said, which was one of the few times she had heard him talk against his wife, so she guessed from that that Lara had been particularly hurtful. 'She was going on, saying she couldn't see what you saw in me, and how she wouldn't mind betting you would drop me as soon as somebody else came along. And —well, to tell the truth, I got a bit rattled, then I remembered the suggestion you put to me that Lara might be upset about our being friends, I remembered I'd scoffed at the idea of her being jealous, but was mad enough to want to try and make her jealous anyway. So I told her it wouldn't matter who else came along because they wouldn't stand a chance because you were in love with me.'

Georgina's spirits weren't any higher when she had finished speaking to Desmond. He had told her if it worried her he would get through to Lara and put up with her laughing at him when he went back on what he had told her. Remembering her own sensitivity to being laughed at, she had told him not to bother. What did it matter anyway? There was very little else that could be hurled at her door that hadn't been hurled already. But if Lara loved Desmond as Tallis had said, then she thought the pair of them wanted their heads banging together for taking every opportunity to wound each other. She had invented an excuse not to see Desmond that night. As fond and as sorry as she was for him, she just couldn't face seeing him, and she half wished she didn't know him so well, didn't know of his loneliness, so she could cut him out of her life altogether and so get some peace from Tallis York and his lashing tongue.

She was grateful that Tallis managed to greet her civilly the next morning. She had dreaded all the way to work a renewal of hostilities that would fray at her nerve ends since she knew he didn't have any meetings today and stood to be constantly in the office. But at least with his, 'Good morning,' he had opened his mouth to do something other than snarl at her, even though 'Georgina' hadn't been tacked on at the end.

'Good morning, T . . .' Her voice tailed off. She thought of him as Tallis now, to change it to Mr York would have a barb of sarcasm coming her way. She seated herself behind her desk reflecting that after yesterday he wouldn't want the familiarity of 'Tallis' coming from her either.

By the time afternoon arrived, she thought a slight thaw had begun to set in. She had been 'Georgina'd' a couple of times throughout the day, though she hadn't called him anything, not out loud anyway, and the names she reserved for him were strictly private.

He was in her office, a piece of paper in his hand, saying, 'Could you . . .' when the phone on her desk rang. He motioned her to answer it, nothing outwardly aggressive showing as he stood looking at her.

But as soon as he realised who her caller was, and her, 'Oh, hello, Desmond,' left him in no doubt about that, his brows came down in a dark frown.

Trying to hang on to the cool sophisticated image that had been with her most of the day, she tried to ignore him as she listened to Desmond asking her out that night. Her heart-strings were pulled to hear the desolation in his voice, but she had done some very serious thinking last night, and had thought that while to stop seeing him altogether wouldn't do him any good, she ought to limit their outings to perhaps one a week. And as the thought bothered her, planted there by Tallis, that she was standing in the way of his reconciliation with Lara, though she still didn't believe it, she would watch for some improvement in Desmond and if an improvement showed itself, she would then stop seeing him except very occasionally.

'Could we give tonight a miss?' she asked him, and seeing a splendid opportunity with Tallis standing there, 'I went away for the weekend and I'm behind with my chores.'

She wished she hadn't looked up then, because expecting at least that Tallis would be giving her a puzzled look, she saw the light of cynicism in his eyes and knew then that he thought she was trying to throw up a smokescreen over the weekend he was convinced she had spent with Desmond.

'Where did you go? Kenilworth?' Desmond asked, knowing of her previous visits.

'Yes,' said Georgina, and left it at that.

'Can you manage tomorrow night, then?' he asked, his voice sounding flat that he had only himself for company that night. 'It's your birthday tomorrow, isn't it—you can't stay at home tomorrow.' Suddenly he seemed to read what was in her mind. 'You're not thinking of ending our friendship, are you?' he asked urgently, sounding all at once so anxious that Georgina just didn't have the heart to be honest with him.

'No, of course not,' she said, injecting lightness where she didn't feel any. 'And since it is my birthday tomorrow, I'm pleased to accept your invitation.'

Tallis had gone back to his own office when she put the phone down. Whatever he had come in to ask her to do couldn't have been important. They were back to the beginning, she realised as she put the cover on her typewriter before going home. He hadn't 'Georgina'd' her once since she had finished speaking to Desmond. Come to think of it, he hadn't spoken to her at all. Georgina didn't speak either. She went home without saying goodnight.

Determined the next morning that nothing was going to upset her day, she got out of bed and opened the parcel Maggie had given her, her spirits lifting when she saw she had perfume from Maggie, talc from Nicola, and hankies from Josh. They had all thought of her, and she felt warmed by their gifts.

Nor did the presents end there, for on going into her office, after a quick flick of her eyes in the direction of Tallis's door to note it was open and that he had arrived before her, she turned her glance quickly away, as he hadn't said good morning, and saw there on her desk a most beautiful vase of carnations.

'Where did ...?' she began involuntarily, and heard Tallis's voice, not hard and nasty as it had been on occasions, but almost light as he called:

'Good morning Georgina—happy birthday.'

'From you?' she asked hesitatingly, referring to the flowers, and wishing she'd left her question unasked.

'Yes, from me,' Tallis confirmed quietly, 'Did you think I was unbearable *all* the time?'

What answer could she give to that? Especially as he had unbent so far from the hateful creature he had been to remember it was her birthday today.

'Thank you,' she said, which didn't answer him at all. 'They're lovely,' she added, and went to take her seat behind her desk.

As the morning progressed, Georgina began to come round to the opinion that as a special birthday treat, Tallis York seemed to be being on his best behaviour today— even to the extent of showing some of the charm she had told Maggie he possessed.

But it was in the early afternoon that she began to doubt

the sincerity of that charm. She had gone into his office with a query, and waited until he looked up, for his desk was covered with calculations and she knew better than to break his train of thought. She looked down at his bent head, saw a strand of grey here and there in his dark hair, and for no reason went off into a dream of what he would look like, say, twenty years from now. He'd still have that certain something then, she thought, that certain something that made him so attractive to women. She paused in her thinking. Was he attractive to women? Don't lie to yourself, Georgina, you know he is. Was *she* attracted to him? Have you forgotten so soon how you felt when he kissed you? How you wanted to respond? jibed her inner voice. Have you forgotten so soon the new discovery you made about yourself? the voice jeered.

'Your thoughts seem to be worrying you, Georgina,' Tallis interrupted her thinking, and she was glad he did so, because she still wasn't very much at home with those sort of thoughts. 'Anything I can help you with?'

His offer seemed genuine enough, but never would he get a whiff of her thoughts from her. She racked her brains to try and recall what she had come into his office for, but it had gone clear out of her head. Then, luckily, she remembered her query and outlined it to him.

'Nothing at all to look so worried about,' Tallis told her, sitting back in his chair as he solved her problem. She turned to go, but he called her back, so she stood with a polite look of enquiry on her face as she waited for him to tell her what he wanted.

'As you can see,' he said, his right hand indicating the paper work on his desk, 'I'm up to my eyes in it today. Would I be asking too much do you think, if I asked you to work late tonight?'

There had been a wealth of charm in his voice. She

knew he was referring to the fact that it was her birthday, and normally it wouldn't have bothered her about working late, but suddenly she was doubting that charm. Suddenly that pleasantly voiced request that she work overtime didn't seem like a request at all. He was ordering her to work late, she saw, and no matter how pleasantly he dressed it up, he was clearly telling her he had found one way of 'sorting her out', for she suspected that his idea of working late didn't mean just working for an hour after five, but longer than that, so there would be no chance of her keeping the date he had heard her make with Desmond yesterday.

'How late is late?' she asked, donning her cool sophisticated air, determined not to refer to the fact that Desmond would be calling for her at eight.

'By the look of this lot here, I shall be lucky if I finish by midnight,' Tallis told her smoothly.

Wondering what he would do if she said no, Georgina looked at him and saw that while that charm was still evident in his face, when she looked at his eyes there was a look of steel there that belied that charm.

'It will be a pleasure to stay and help you,' she said sweetly, trying for some of his phoney charm, only her charm not deceiving him in the least.

The door between the two offices had remained open for most of the day, but Georgina closed it as she went back into her own office. If she was going to have to ring Desmond and cancel their date, then she wanted to do it in private.

At eight o'clock that night her head was spinning from the amount of work they had got through since the rest of the staff had gone home. She was having a hard time to keep Tallis from seeing she was flagging, and she began to feel resentful that he didn't show any signs of the weariness she was feeling. His pace hadn't slackened any, and yet he had been in the office before her that morning. She was starving, and thought of the meal she should have been eating with Desmond, wondering if she would have either the energy or inclination to cook herself something when she eventually made it to her flat.

At ten to nine, when she was fast growing to the opinion that when Tallis had said he'd be lucky if he finished before midnight, he hadn't been joking, he suddenly tossed his pen aside and said:

'That's it—let's go and eat.'

'Eat?' Georgina questioned.

'Neither of us have had dinner, and you know you won't bother with anything more than a cheese sandwich if I don't feed you.'

As an invitation to dine, Georgina had received better phrased ones, but suddenly the idea of just sitting down and having a plate of food set before her presented much too much of a temptation to resist.

Tallis took her to an Italian restaurant, and they spoke very little as, both famished, they got down to the business of eating. It was as they were drinking their coffee that Tallis told her he wouldn't be in at all the next day.

'Thanks for your help tonight,' he said. 'I dislike leaving work outstanding, and I shall need some of those calculations for tomorrow.'

'But you could have managed without me tonight, couldn't you?' Having been fed, Georgina felt more equal to doing battle.

'Would you have rested easy knowing I was burning the midnight oil?'

Would she not! 'Always pleased to be of assistance,' she said, and idiotically, when she meant to let him see she didn't think much of his method of keeping her away from Desmond, she felt like grinning.

She didn't grin, of course. But Tallis did. And she was glad at that point that the waiter came to offer more coffee. For seeing Tallis grin like that had caused the oddest of reactions in her heart region. Indigestion, I expect, she thought as she declined more coffee, though she could never remember suffering from indigestion before.

It was nearer eleven than ten when Tallis dropped her off at her front door. He got out of the car and stood with her on the pavement for a moment as Georgina thanked him nicely for her meal. Then, just as she was about to turn and go up the stone steps to the front door, he said, as he had done first thing that morning:

'Happy birthday,' and while she searched for something to say, though all that was required, she realised afterwards, was 'goodnight', she felt his arms come round her and his head was coming down, and he kissed her firmly on her mouth before pushing her just as firmly away from him. 'Goodnight, Georgina,' he said, and was going back to his car.

'G-goodnight,' she threw over her shoulder, and hurried to the door, not turning round but opening the door and going through. She stood silently for a few seconds, listened for the sound of his car starting up, and only then did she move away from the door.

As every day she had spent at Chestertons had been busy, the next day was no exception, and Georgina was grateful for it. She didn't want to think about that birthday kiss Tallis had given her last night.

Her working day ended with a tape full of messages for him, though Naomi Garrick hadn't rung; she hadn't rung yesterday either, come to think of it. Georgina found herself humming a little tune as she covered her typewriter.

She told herself it was pleasing to feel one had done a good day's work.

After having her meal and attending to the washing up, she was free to have a nice long chat with her family in Kenilworth. She always wrote to them once a week, but had intended to ring last night to thank them for her presents, though she had thought Nicola and Josh would be in bed when Tallis brought her home and she would be too late to speak with them.

Anticipating hearing Maggie's bubbly overtones coming across the wire, she knew instantly that something was wrong. Oh, Maggie was making every effort to sound cheerful and was succeeding, only to Georgina's ears she was sounding too cheerful, and she thought she detected strain in Maggie's voice the longer the conversation went on.

Georgina thanked her for her gift, and learning that both Nicola and Josh were out, asked Maggie to pass on her thanks to them for the talc and handkerchiefs.

'Did you go somewhere nice last night?' Maggie enquired. 'I thought when you didn't ring you would be out celebrating.'

Georgina knew Maggie wasn't censuring her for not ringing, but she had the growing certainty that Maggie had expected her to call last night, and had been ready then as she was now to try and fool her with a false air of cheerfulness.

'What's wrong, Maggie?' she asked quietly.

'Wrong? Why—er—nothing.'

That didn't ring true—that hesitation before she said 'nothing'. 'You're worried about something.' Her mind went over all possibilities while she listened to Maggie stressing, too heavily she thought, that everything was fine. Money was the first thing that came to mind, though Maggie was used to managing on a tight budget. Perhaps

Nicola or Josh needed something new that Maggie just couldn't afford. About to question her on this and ready to use all the tact she could muster to say she would get it whatever it was—that new dress she was saving for could wait another couple of months—something Maggie had said earlier came back, and she was sure then that whatever it was that had put that note of strain into Maggie's voice, it was something to do with Josh. Maggie had said both Nicola *and* Josh were out. It was a long-standing family joke that except for Mondays, you couldn't get Josh to budge until he had done his homework, and at this time of night his head was always buried deep in his books.

'What has Josh been up to, Maggie?' she asked, knowing it must be something out of the norm to have taken Maggie out of her unflappable stride, for all she was trying to cover it.

There was an astonished silence at the other end, then Maggie was almost gasping, 'How did you know?'

So it was Josh! 'Please tell me, Maggie, I won't get a wink of sleep tonight unless I know.' And if that wouldn't coax it out of her! 'I shall come home first thing tomorrow if you don't—Tonight if . . .'

That did the trick. Reluctantly Maggie began to tell her everything, reminding her of the chat they'd had last Sunday about her unmarried state when they had both thought Josh outside overhauling Nicola's bike. Only he hadn't been outside all the time. He had come back into the house to ask, in the absence of a small screwdriver, if he could borrow Maggie's nail file, but had been arrested by what they were saying when he had reached the living room door.

Maggie's voice had dropped its pretence of being cheerful, her voice was now toneless as she went on, and Georg-

ina knew there was a welter of worry behind her now flat
tones. 'Josh is adamant he's leaving school at the end of
term,' she said. 'He says he's not having you sacrifice
your life for him.'

'Oh, Maggie . . .' Georgina began, horrified.

'I know, I know. I've given him all the arguments you
gave me, but you know he always thinks everything out,
and he's taken it into his head to believe you're in love
with someone, but that you won't allow it to go any further
because you know we can't manage without the help you
give us.' There was a break in Maggie's voice as she went
on, for all she tried to conceal it, and Georgina could have
wept as she heard it. 'He's turned his back on the idea of
going to university.' Maggie paused and Georgina was sure
she was swallowing her tears before, once more in control,
she continued, 'He's determined to leave school and get a
job—and . . . and I just can't talk him out of it.'

Georgina wrestled with the problem of Josh all that
evening, knowing that to go to Kenilworth to talk to him
wouldn't do any good. If Maggie couldn't convince him,
she wasn't going to be able to, unless she could come up
with something brilliant his clever young brain wouldn't
set about dissecting.

She slept only fitfully, and wasn't surprised next morning to see that her eyes looked tired, her face washed out.
But with her mind heavy with worry over Josh, what her
face looked like was the least of her problems.

Tallis hadn't arrived when she reached the office, and
her mind was not in any way on her work when the door
opened ten minutes later. When she raised her troubled
eyes to see him there, she had no idea how long he had
been standing there surveying her.

'Er—good morning,' she said, abruptly, leaving her
private thoughts as he closed the door and walked to the

front of her desk. It was going to be another of those days, she could tell from the glowering look he was favouring her with. No answering greeting was forthcoming, and that kiss he had given her the night before last could never have been as he continued to give her silent scrutiny.

'You look as though you hadn't been to bed,' he observed, then, his tone sharp, 'Or is that the trouble? You did go to bed—accompanied?'

The spurt of temper that shot through her at his insulting remark, was the first spark of life she had felt since she had awakened that morning. Wanting to tell him to go to hell, she bit back her anger.

'Sour grapes because you didn't fare so well?' she asked sweetly, and swallowed quickly, drawing back out of range when a look of such fury crossed his face that she appeared to be admitting what he had accused her of, she thought he was going to hit her. Then from a long way off, control seemed to come to him, and without another word his jaw clenched hard, and he turned to march through into his own office.

Several times during the next couple of hours, when her mind had gone repeatedly backwards and forwards to Josh, Georgina would look up and find Tallis watching her through the open door, a none too pleasant look on his face. She tried to keep her own face expressionless because she didn't want to give him any idea that she was worried only for him to put his own construction on why she was worried. She wasn't in the mood for any of his barbed remarks about Desmond and didn't trust herself not to tell the chairman of Chestertons to go to hell yet, if he had calculated that the only thing she was worried about was her 'affair' with Desmond.

Tallis strode past her desk just after eleven, and not sure if he intended coming back and wanting to know what to tell his callers, she asked quickly before he disappeared, quite probably for the rest of the day, 'Will you be back?' and watched while he turned and gave her a look that asked what the devil it had to do with her, before he seemed to realise why she wanted to know.

'Not for a couple of hours,' he told her coldly, and went out.

She really would look in the situations vacant column tonight, Georgina thought. By the sound of it she was going to have to put up with him for the whole of the afternoon. She then forgot all about Tallis York, as thoughts of Josh returned to worry her.

Georgina took her hour off at lunch time, but had never felt less like eating. She attempted a sandwich, but left half of it, though she drained her coffee cup before thinking it was time she made her way back to the office. *He* wasn't back yet, so that was a blessing, she thought, as she pulled her typewriter towards her. She began to type, then recalled that Tallis had said he would be out for a couple of hours. That meant he could possibly have come while she was at lunch, done some work and then gone out to his own lunch. She stopped typing. Better see if he had left her anything on tape.

She stretched her hand to the tape machine and switched it on, knowing it was his custom to wind it back to where he had begun. Her hand was still outstretched to the machine when the outer door opened. Disbelievingly she stared at the tall, thin young man who had just come in, her fingers going automatically to switch off the machine, and then everything else went out of her mind.

'*Josh!*' she exclaimed, getting to her feet. 'What on earth are you doing here?'

CHAPTER SEVEN

GEORGINA was too shocked at seeing her stepbrother, school blazer and flannels-clad, standing there, to move once her initial start had got her out of her chair. And Josh, mistaking her shock, was by her side in a few lanky strides, his serious young face concerned as he asked:

'Is it all right for me to come to your office? I don't want to get you into trouble, but I had to see you, Georgie.'

'Of course it's all right,' Georgina told him, getting over her surprise and hastening to reassure him. 'I just didn't expect to see you, that's all.' She smiled warmly at him. 'What are you doing in London, though?' she asked, thinking his class must have come up to some exhibition, while her mind grew anxious if he had sloped off without his master noticing and thinking of the trouble he would be in when he went back. 'Have you come with the school . . .' she started to say.

'I haven't been to school today,' he told her, the way he was looking down at his shoes letting her know more than he knew, because Josh was never afraid to look the person he was speaking with in the eye.

'Oh, Josh!' she exclaimed, her anxiety going in another direction. Josh never missed a day's school if he could help it. She knew then that this visit had some purpose, and was not just the result of some schoolboy mischief.

'I had to see you, Georgie,' Josh said again, excusing his truancy. Then as though he wanted to get what had been stewing inside him off his chest, and quickly, he went straight into the reason for his playing truant. 'Mum told me she'd told you on the phone last night about me, and I knew you'd be worrying too.'

What a dear boy he was, she thought. He took his responsibilities much too seriously, but she could see from the look of him he wasn't going to feel any better until he had tried to make her see his point of view.

'Listen to me, Josh,' she said. Much as she wanted to make him feel better, she intended to go to the heart of the matter. Determined, since he was here, to do all she could to make him change his viewpoint. 'There's absolutely no need for you to leave school at the end of term. I told Maggie on ...'

'Oh, Georgie,' he interrupted her painfully, 'please don't give me the same hog wash you gave Mum. I've had days to think over all I overheard you telling her last Sunday, and it just doesn't equate.'

Oh, why, oh, why couldn't Josh just accept what he had heard? Georgina thought despairingly, trying to remember everything she had told Maggie, but knowing full well it was just because Josh's young mind was already so analytical that such a brilliant future had been forecast for him.

'It was all true, Josh,' she lied desperately. 'Every word I told ...'

'That you're not married because the right man hasn't asked you?' he interrupted again, remembering, Georgina thought, better than she had every sentence that had passed between Maggie and her.

'That's right,' she said, then going very carefully, 'You're young yet, Josh, so you won't know much about the opposite sex. But—but when you're older you'll know for yourself that you just don't marry because—because it's expected of you. If—if you don't find mutual love—well, then you just stay single. Honestly, darling,' she went on, hoping she was sounding as convincing to Josh as she did in her own ears, 'you've blown this thing up out of all proportion. You ...'

'You're saying you haven't found that mutual love yet?' he asked, ploughing determinedly on, for all he looked to be a shade pink to be discussing the emotion called love with his grown-up stepsister.

Georgina smiled gently at him, aware of his embarrassment. Then a thought suddenly struck her, and she knew she would have to go even more carefully, as realisation grew, and with it hope, that much as Josh didn't want her to worry, it seemed that by his very act of coming to London to see her, he might be looking to be convinced that what his brain had deduced from her conversation with his mother might yet not be so.

'Look, Josh, perhaps I wasn't being as truthful as I should have been with your mother on Sunday, but it was a shock to me to learn that Maggie had been worrying about me at all. So when I did know, I didn't want to give her anything further to worry over me about, so I didn't tell her the whole truth.'

'The whole truth!' Josh came in quickly. 'You mean Mum *was* right when she said she thought you were sacrificing ...'

'No, no, I don't mean that at all,' Georgina butted in hastily, wanting to get him away from all thoughts sursounding the word sacrifice. 'You and I were talking about people falling in love ...'

'You said it was a two-sided thing,' Josh back-tracked, and she could almost see his bright young brain ticking over as he fell silent for a moment or two and sifted through what she had told him before coming up with the conclusion she wanted him to. 'Are you saying that

you love somebody, but that he doesn't want to marry
you? Is that it?' he brought out.

Bless his intelligence, Georgina thought. 'That's it exactly,' she said, stifling the excitement in her and trying
to look a mite downcast. If she could get Josh to believe her
love wasn't returned, then while the years passed with
him studying, with any luck he would think the reason she
was still single was because she was still suffering from the
pangs of unrequited love. As he got older, more aware,
perhaps he would think that his stepsister was the kind of
girl who only ever gave her heart once.

She was shaken out of her renewed dream for his future
to see that pink flush of embarrassment cross his face once
more, and to realise that at nearly seventeen, Josh wasn't
as unworldly as she had supposed.

'This man—this man you say you're in love with,
Georgie. Is he already married?'

The idea was with her to say yes. That way seemed
much the safer if Josh was to have any future doubts. But
for all his question showed a growing maturity in him, his
blush reminded her of her previous thought. Josh wasn't
seventeen yet—she just couldn't bring herself to let him
think she had fallen for someone who already had a wife; it
just didn't taste nice.

'No, Josh, he's not married. He just doesn't know I exist.'
It was irksome to her that a picture of Tallis York glowering at her that morning should come to mind, but it was a
reminder that he could come in at any moment. She looked
at her watch and made a decision. 'There's a café nearby,
shall we go and find a cup of tea? We can talk in comfort
there.'

Josh waited while she picked up her bag, in agreement
for some refreshment, but telling her he would have to
watch the time because in order that his mother shouldn't

be more worried than she was already, he hadn't said he was cutting school and that if possible he wanted to catch a train that would get him home at his usual time. Georgina was hopeful that when he did arrive home he would be telling Maggie something that would take a load of worry from her.

It was going on for four when a much happier Georgina returned to Chestertons. She glanced at Tallis's door and hearing no sound thought it must be her lucky day after all. Tallis wasn't back yet, she hadn't been missed. Not that she worried about the time she had taken off, she had worked late enough on Wednesday to more than make up for it, she just didn't want to have to dream up an excuse for her absence, that was all.

Her mind went over her conversation with Josh before she'd gone with him in a taxi to the station. He had put her through a sticky half hour, she had to admit, and she marvelled at the logic of his questions. But at the end of that half an hour she thought she had finally got through to him that he would be letting her down badly if he left school now. She was fairly confident too that he no longer believed she was making any sacrifice for him. And although he hadn't given her his word to go back on his decision, she had every faith that when he had dissected everything she had told him—as she knew he would—then he, or Maggie, would be getting in touch with her soon to say he had done so.

Now, where had she been before Josh had shattered her by coming in through that door? Ah, yes, she'd been about to see what Tallis had left for her on tape, she'd better get on with some work. Switching on the tape machine, she heard not a thing. Then thinking that had Tallis recorded anything he might have forgotten to wind it back, she spun the tape back, then forward again. She'd turned it back too far, she realised as she heard the message she had recorded just before lunch.

She waited, expecting that the next voice she heard, if any, would be Tallis giving her some instruction, then was astounded to hear her own voice exclaiming, 'Josh! What on earth are you doing here?' followed by her stepbrother's voice asking if it was all right for him to call at her office. Straightaway she realised what she had done. So shaken to see Josh standing there, her fingers had gone blindly for the off switch, but instead she had switched on to record.

She listened to the tape, but there was no instruction from Tallis tacked on to the end, so he couldn't have popped back. Well, that was a relief. He could so easily have come in and turned the tape back as she had done. She didn't want him listening in to her private conversations.

Her relief wavered as she thought she heard a sound from his office. Imagination, of course, but she was at Tallis's door without knowing it. Certain she had imagined the noise, she turned the handle without bothering to knock, a courtesy she would normally have employed in case he had someone with him, and pushed the door inwards.

Her eyes met night-black eyes full on, and the only emotion she felt then was heaving disquiet. For there, looking relaxed, in command, and no longer glowering as he had been that morning, sat Tallis York taking careful note of the uneasiness in her expression as it came to her that it would be second nature to him to check for messages when he came in.

'Er . . .' she struggled, when he seemed quite content to look at her without offering up any comment. 'Er—I'm sorry I wasn't here when you got back.' Still no comment. And then Georgina's jumbled thoughts sorted themselves out, and with the hope that perhaps Tallis had only just come in and had not yet got round to listening to his messages, she forced herself to appear outwardly calm at any rate, and added, with an attempt at coolness, 'I had to go out for a while.'

Her façade of coolness vanished abruptly when Tallis did deign to speak.

'Josh caught his train all right, did he?' he enquired, and as her deeply blue eyes grew wide in her face, he instructed her, 'Sit down, Georgina. It would appear I owe you an apology.'

Georgina was glad to sit down. 'Apology?' she queried, wondering what he was going to apologise for. Not that there weren't a dozen things she could think of he should be sorry for. But most likely, it came to her, he was going to apologise for accidentally overhearing her conversation with Josh. 'I didn't know I'd switched the machine on to record. I thought I'd switched it off.'

'The "On" light was showing when I came in,' Tallis told her, 'I thought you'd left a message to say where you'd gone.'

If she had been expecting him to apologise for not switching off as soon as he realised it was a private conversation, and she knew he had heard all of it, because nothing had been mentioned about Josh catching a train until the very end, then she was very much mistaken, for in the next breath Tallis was saying:

'I found your conversation most interesting—not to say enlightening.' Which was no sort of an apology, she thought, as he looked ready to discuss several of the points he had picked up. 'Who is Josh, by the way?'

'My stepbrother,' she replied, when she had already made up her mind she wasn't entering into any discussion with him about anything he had heard.

'And a very worried stepbrother, I'd say,' Tallis opined before she could tell him it was none of his business. Her family were very private to her, even Desmond didn't know of their circumstances. 'Does he often play truant from school?'

'No,' Georgina said stoutly, her intention to get up and march back to her own office forestalled by the need to defend young Josh. 'Normally he's dedicated to his studies, but—but as you said, he was worried about—something.'

The look on her face told him she'd have to be put on the rack before he would get her talking about the worries of her stepbrother. 'He must be over sixteen to be able to leave school,' Tallis said after looking at her consideringly.

'He's almost seventeen,' she found herself staying to say.

'Why is it so important that he stay on at school?' Tallis asked thoughtfully.

And it was her pride in Josh. Pride pure and simple that had her still sitting there, a warm look on her face, as she told Tallis, 'Josh has a first-class brain. He's set his heart on being a doctor. Our ... Maggie's plans for him would be ruined if he left school now.'

'Since Josh is your stepbrother, I presume Maggie is your stepmother,' Tallis tidied up before continuing. 'It seems you've all had a worrying time. Josh thought you'd be worrying too after you'd spoken with his mother on the phone last night.'

She didn't answer. Whether she and members of her family worried or not was nothing to do with him. And anyway, this conversation had gone on for far too long as far as she was concerned. She then looked at Tallis and thought she saw that glint of steel appear in his eyes, and knew she should have left when she had intended to.

'It was worrying that caused you to look tired this morning,' he stated. 'It had nothing to do with Warner, had it?'

Georgina rose to her feet. She hadn't liked discussing her family with Tallis. She particularly didn't want Desmond to enter into it, for it seemed to her that whenever his name came up, she and Tallis invariably ended up having a row, or if not a row, then a cold war seemed to be the natural aftermath.

'I didn't see Desmond last night,' she stated flatly, and made to leave, only to find Tallis had stood up too and had come to block her way.

'You didn't go away with him for the weekend either, did you,' he stated, when on Monday he hadn't even given her the benefit of the doubt.

And it made her mad that he should need to hear Josh refer to her talking to Maggie on Sunday before he changed his ideas. It made her mad that he hadn't been prepared to listen to her on Monday, but now, when his deductions told him that Desmond couldn't have accompanied her otherwise Josh would have mentioned him, only now was he ready to listen. And it made her madder still that if this was Tallis York's way of apologising for being such a pig on Monday then she felt very let down by it. Well, she didn't intend telling him anything. Gathering all the sophistication she could around her, she looked him coolly in the eye and said loftily:

'Beginning to doubt your source of information?' neither agreeing nor denying the innocence of her weekend. 'Surely you're not beginning to doubt that I'm not the marriage breaker you think I am?'

He didn't like her tone, she could see that, but she refused to weaken in her stance as a hard look came over his face.

'No way,' he said grittily, then challenged, 'I have the evidence of my own eyes, haven't I?' And when he saw she had no reply to make to that, 'Deny your affair with Warner as much as you like,' he grated, 'but don't try a whitewash job with me. I myself saw Warner leaving your flat early one morning before you'd had time to get dressed.'

Her armour was badly dented at that remark, but she kept her chin held high. She had done nothing she need be ashamed of, but was past wanting to explain that Desmond had only popped in for his briefcase that morning. She wouldn't forget in a hurry the unpleasant remarks Tallis had made that day. At that moment he moved, clearing her way to the door. Unspeaking, she went to go past him, she had nothing she wanted to say to him and couldn't wait to close the door between the two offices with her on the other side.

But if she had nothing more she wanted to say to him, then her very silence seemed to rouse further unwanted remarks from him. 'I'd have thought you'd have had more guts,' he said icily as she opened the door. 'I'd have thought you could have confessed to your stepmother and stepbrother the real reason you haven't married yet.'

Involuntarily she turned, saw from his contemptuous look that he didn't think very much of her, but after that first quick start of panic she realised he couldn't possibly know she had decided not to get involved with any man until Josh and Nicola had been educated.

'And what reason would that be?' she asked, trying to hang on to her lofty pose, but not managing it very well, she thought, in the face of his disgust.

'The truth, Georgina Underwood,' he said, and turned from her, giving her a good idea that he considered he had more important things to do than to wrangle with the likes of her. 'But then,' he added, sitting down and picking up his pen in an obvious dismissing gesture, 'you haven't that kind of honesty in you, have you? The honesty that de-

mands you tell your family that the man you want to
marry is already married, and likely to stay that way.'

All of Friday night and all day Saturday, Georgina waited
for the phone to ring. Waited for that call from Kenilworth that would tell her Josh would be staying on at
school. She almost rang through herself when the waiting
began to get her down, but forced herself not to jump the
gun. It would be all too easy to overplay her hand. She
was convinced Josh would be thinking it all out, and one
false move on her part could ruin everything.

She did have one phone call on Saturday, but that was
from Desmond, asking her out. She went out with him
that night, but not until after nine o'clock when she was
certain Maggie would think her out anyway, and neither
she nor Josh would ring after that time.

She thought Desmond looked much improved, and she
was pleased to see him more cheerful than he had been.
When he told her about a business dinner he had been
invited to on Monday, and how he was expected to take a
partner, she readily agreed to go with him, suspecting he
would doubly feel his loneliness if he was the only one
without a partner.

There was no telephone call from Kenilworth on Sunday, and again she had to hold back the urge to ring herself. By the time Monday morning arrived, the strain of
waiting was beginning to show in her face.

Tallis greeted her civilly enough, but she saw his shrewd
eyes on her more than once when there was a break in his
dictation. She was again in his office checking through
some correspondence when half way through the morning
a messenger brought up a bouquet of flowers for her. Tallis
immediately stopped work, and barely waited for the messenger to close the outer door before he was saying nastily:

'Warner saying it with flowers?'

Georgina ignored him, her fingers busy searching for the card. Desmond had never sent her flowers, there was no reason at all why he should start now, but who else ... She found the card, blank side first, then turned it over.

The flowers weren't from Desmond, and she could have wept that Josh must have spent several weeks' pocket money to soften the blow of what the message on the card told her. 'Don't be angry with me, Georgie,' she read, and she could do nothing to hold back the groan of, 'Oh no!' that was wrung from her or to stop the tears that sprang to her eyes, as she realised that all her hopeful waiting this weekend had ended with Josh not going back on his decision.

'What is it?' Tallis asked, leaving his chair and coming to seat himself on the corner of his desk near her. The despair in her 'Oh no!' hadn't missed him, and he could see for himself the battle she was having not to break down completely in front of him.

Then before she could stop him, he had taken the card from her hands, noting that the sender of the daffodils, jonquils and tulips was not Desmond Warner, before he read the message. And then Georgina saw a very different Tallis from the one she thought she knew. She felt her hand taken in his as very gently he asked, 'Care to tell me what this is all about?'

Georgina looked up at him, touched by the gentleness in his tone and swallowing hard as control over·her emotions at that moment was anywhere but with her. 'Oh, Tallis,' she said huskily, felt a tear on her cheek and wiped it hastily away with the back of her hand.

'This has something to do with Josh leaving school, hasn't it?' he probed, still on that same gentle note that was doing nothing to brace her.

'I th-thought when I said goodbye to him on Friday that I'd be hearing from him that he'd decided to stay at school after all,' she said, Tallis's gentle urging, her dashed hopes for Josh, the despair of her feelings, all loosening her tongue. 'I've waited and waited all weekend for a telephone call to say he'd reconsidered his decision to leave school—I was so s-sure on Friday he would.'

'Isn't there a man in the house to talk some sense into him?' Tallis queried.

'Josh's father died when he was small. My father died five years ago ,' she told him abstractedly.

'So at sixteen this young man makes all the decisions in the household, does he?'

Had Tallis asked that question sharply, or in any way in a tone of voice she was more used to, she would have clammed up right there. But there was no sharpness in him, just a gentle questioning, sounding so much as though he was really interested, as though he wanted to help, and for all she knew there was nothing he could do to help, she found herself answering:

'He's at an age where he's forming his own opinions, developing his character. Maggie had done a splendid job with him singlehanded since my father died,' she said, and then, when at any other time nothing would have dragged it from her, she found, to her astonishment afterwards, that she was confessing, 'But there isn't very much money to spare and Josh thinks—thinks it would be better if he got a job.'

'On Friday he referred to you sacrificing something,' Tallis said slowly. Then, his voice changing very slightly as if he was making a great effort to keep the hardness out of it, 'You told him then that you were in love, but that the recipient of your affections didn't know you existed—there's a tie-up somewhere, isn't there?' And when she didn't answer, he pressed on, 'Josh thinks you're making some sacrifice for him,' and talking his thoughts through, since it seemed Georgina had said as much as she was going to, 'He overheard you telling his mother that you weren't married because the right man hadn't asked you. So the sacrifice the boy believes you're making has something to do with you being unmarried.'

Georgina knew at that point that Tallis would get there on his own with no help from her, but it seemed to her then that she wouldn't be able to take it, if in getting to the right conclusion he went off course and referred again, as he had on Friday, to her single state being because Desmond wasn't free. She didn't think she was up to taking anything he had to say on the subject of her 'affair' with Desmond on top of everything else. So before he could make any further connections, she found her voice and told him wearily:

'I send a cheque home every month. Maggie thought, and Josh thinks, that I'm keeping all men at arm's length because if I were to marry—to give up my job, then ...'

'Then the support you give them would cease,' Tallis put in, and the hand holding hers squeezed her fingers in instant understanding. 'You're paid better than many secretaries,' he added thoughtfully. 'Is that why you were so desperate to keep your job, when the look in your eyes that first day we met told me you'd like to tell me exactly what I could do with it?'

'Y-yes,' Georgina whispered, and lifted sad eyes to look at him. The gentleness in him wasn't limited to his voice, she saw, for the look in his eyes was gentle too.

'You're a sweetie, Georgina,' he told her. Then while she sat there slightly stunned to hear such a comment coming her way from him, he leaned forward and kissed her gently on the mouth.

Instinctively she pulled back, but not before it came to her that there had been comfort in the feel of his lips on hers, and she wouldn't have minded a scrap at that moment if he had taken her in his arms and comforted her some more. Amazed by the turn her thoughts were taking, she pulled her hand out of his hold.

'I'd—I'd better go and put these in water,' she said, her teeth nibbling at her bottom lip as her eyes returned to the card Tallis had placed on the desk.

'Try not to worry,' he urged her. 'We'll think of something that will have that young man having his university education.'

'We!' Georgina exclaimed.

Tallis grinned, the second grin she could remember coming her way from him, and unaccountably her heart began to pump faster. 'I can't have my secretary weeping all over my correspondence, can I?' he teased, then seriously, he urged her again, 'Don't worry, there's a good girl.'

Back at her desk, Georgina found that being told not to worry was easier said than done. Constantly during the next hour her thoughts flitted back to Josh, wondering what else she could do to make him change his mind, but she was unable to come up with anything. Tallis York occupied a good deal of her thoughts too, for she had never suspected that gentle, almost tender side to him.

It was after lunch, the anxiety in her mind none the easier, that a man of about sixty entered her office and temporarily kept her worries at bay. She had never seen the man before and didn't much take to the cold look he gave her through his thick-lensed glasses. Nonetheless, she was prepared to smile politely ready to ask what he wanted —only to find he didn't smile back but went striding past her desk to Tallis's office.

Getting to her feet, she went to go after him to tell him

he just couldn't walk through like that without an appointment. But she was too late, he had the door open and before she could get to him, not bothering to lower his voice, she heard him say:

'Is that the Underwood woman, Tallis?' What Tallis said she didn't hear, but he must have confirmed it, for the next thing she heard the man say was, 'I don't know how you can keep that woman working here. Don't family loyalties count for anything with you?' The door closed, and she knew then exactly who Tallis's visitor was.

Lara's father was with Tallis for over an hour, during which time Georgina had got over the shock of being looked at so unfavourably by a man she had never met. But now, added to her desperation at trying to think of some way to talk Josh round, she was experiencing renewed disquiet that for all Tallis had promised he wouldn't dismiss her, from the slighting way Edgar Rankin had spoken of her she could be pretty sure he was again having another go at getting Tallis to change his mind.

When the door did eventually open, she went purposefully on with her typing. She had no intention of looking at Edgar Rankin again and receiving another of his black looks. But when both Tallis and his uncle came through the door and Tallis halted his uncle by her desk, she just had to look up. And she stopped work altogether when she heard Tallis say:

'You haven't met Georgina, have you?' Her hands came away from her typewriter and she just didn't know how she kept her surprise from showing when Tallis turned to her and said easily, 'You know of my uncle, of course, darling.'

How she managed to keep her jaw from dropping, Georgina didn't know. But her surprise was more from the 'darling', she thought, rather than from the impudence of Tallis actually introducing her to his uncle, who she was certain would much prefer to ignore her than shake her hand.

Edgar Rankin did not ignore her, but seemed to be making every effort to be polite by stretching out his hand. What she answered to his brief, 'How do you do,' she had no idea, and then Tallis was escorting his uncle to the other door, passing a few comments with him, then after seeing him out, was coming back to prop himself against her desk near her.

'What was all that about?' she gasped before he could speak. 'If looks could have killed when he came in I'd be dead by now. I thought the very last thing he would do would be to shake hands with me.'

Tallis leaned forward and brushed a fleck of cotton off the sleeve of her blouse before answering, then, his eyes going to her bewildered face, 'Can't think,' he said casually. 'Though it could have something to do with the fact I told him you were no longer seeing Warner. That you're now my girl-friend.'

'Your girl-friend!' Georgina gasped, her eyes glued to his dark ones for proof that she had heard him correctly. Then, not knowing what game he was playing, but sure she wasn't going to like it whatever it was, she stated coldly, 'That just isn't true, and anyway, I'm still seeing Desmond —I'm having dinner with him tonight, as a matter of fact.'

She saw a hardness enter his eyes at that, but the rest of him stayed casual as slowly he shook his head.

'No, you're not.' Then, his casual air dropping away from him, he told her forcefully, 'You're not seeing Warner tonight or any other night.'

The cheek of the man! she thought, gasping afresh at the cool audacity of him. 'Oh yes, I am,' she began, growing heated. 'I shall see Desmond as often as I jolly well like!'

'Even if it means you can tell your stepbrother you're going steady with someone who has sufficient funds so that when you marry you'll still be able to send your monthly cheque home without feeling the pinch?'

'Marry!' Georgina echoed, as fresh shock waves hit her.

'Neither of us need go to such drastic lengths,' Tallis told her sharply, reading from her shocked face that he would be the last one she would think of as a husband, and she knew from 'drastic lengths' that marriage with her was the last thing he had in mind. 'I told you this morning I'd think of something. It seems to me to be an excellent solution to both our problems. I can give you the cover you need while Josh gets on with his studies, and in return, by letting it be known that you're my girl, the heat will be taken off me to get rid of you.'

Georgina was silent as her thoughts fought for precedence. It was difficult not to get excited that she could tell Josh that the man she loved had proposed after all, that problems of money just wouldn't figure. There wouldn't be one single argument he could raise. He could finish his education. He would never know she wasn't even going out with Tallis, much less thinking of marrying him.

Her excitement died a little as she looked up and found Tallis closely watching her. He had spoken of the heat being taken off him to get rid of her if she agreed, and her heart quailed that, as she had thought, Tallis was again being pressured to break his word to her.

Knowing she should be snatching his hand off for the cover he was offering, something within her made her argue, 'I can't see with all the pressures I've seen you cope with, that you couldn't handle any pressure your uncle applies to have me dismissed.'

'You've forgotten family loyalties,' Tallis answered. 'You, I think, know something of loyalty to one's family. You heard Edgar turning the screw when he came in about what he believes is my disloyalty to himself and Lara.'

A flutter of panic rose within her. He wasn't pulling any punches. She knew enough about him to know he would hate breaking his word. But placed in the same position, keeping a promise or keeping her family happy, which would she do?

'You've—er—no objection to me telling Josh that you and I are—er . . .'

'Going to be married,' Tallis supplied. Then practically, 'I can't see that young man swallowing any other tale—since you don't feel able to tell him the real truth.'

That hard note again. It seemed they just couldn't have any discussion without Desmond coming into it. And the real truth as Tallis saw it was that she had no intention of marrying anyone unless it was Desmond. Thinking of Desmond had her recalling that Tallis had coolly announced she wouldn't be seeing Desmond tonight or any other night.

'Desmond . . .' she said involuntarily, unable to help worrying what it would do to him if he didn't have her to use as a lifeline, but seeing from the way Tallis's lips tightened at his name that if Josh's future wasn't to be sacrificed, then her friendship with Desmond was going to have to be.

'You'd better get in touch with him, hadn't you?' said Tallis, getting up from the corner of her desk.

'To tell him I won't see him tonight, do you mean?'

He gave her a cool look which she read as saying, 'or ever', then without speaking he went into his office and closed his door.

Georgina supposed, grudgingly, she should be grateful that he had closed his door. The job before her was not going to be easy. Though as she dialled Desmond's number, she realised she shouldn't grudge Tallis anything.

Without the idea he had come up with, without his willingness to be a partner in this deception, she would still be sitting here fretting herself silly over Josh.

Desmond was not pleased that she was calling their date off, and weak though she knew she was being, when she recognised that note in his voice that told her he was feeling very low, she just couldn't find it in her heart to tell him she wouldn't be seeing him again. She replaced the phone knowing she had been cowardly to put off telling him until he sounded in a brighter frame of mind. As it was, he hadn't taken very well the excuse that some urgent work had come up and she wouldn't be finished until it was too late for her to accompany him as his dinner partner.

She was on the point of going home when Tallis's door opened and he came through. 'It occurred to me that since I've deprived you of the meal you were going to have with Warner tonight, I'd better take you to dinner myself,' he announced baldly.

Georgina's eyebrows ascended at the cheek of him. She swallowed down her wrath while wondering that he could still so easily make her temper rise when she considered the very enormous favour he was doing her. 'That's very kind of you,' she said coolly, 'but I can assure you I shan't go hungry if I don't accept.'

As her brows had ascended, so at her refusal did his brows come darkly down. 'You didn't phone Warner,' he accused. 'You still intend having dinner with him. Well, let me tell you, Miss Underwood ...'

'Of course I phoned him,' she interrupted hastily, ready, should he ask, to agree to dine with him every night of the week when it looked very much as if he was furious enough to cancel their agreement, looked furious enough to break his word about her job and wash his hands of everything to do with her. 'It's just that I—I want to ring Maggie tonight, only—only I want to do it when Josh is there, and he always goes straight from school to play chess with some of his friends on Mondays. He won't be home until about half past eight.'

For one ghastly moment she thought he was convinced she was lying. Then the fury died from his face. 'I see,' was all he said.

Georgina's racing heart settled to a normal beat. She picked up her bag and went home.

CHAPTER EIGHT

IT seemed to Georgina, as she waited until she thought that Josh would be home, that half past eight would never arrive. Countless times as the minutes dragged by she rehearsed what she was going to say. Maggie too had to be lied to, had to be convinced, and she must make her voice sound happy, as though she was on top of the world. None of the tension she was feeling must be allowed to be heard.

At twenty-seven minutes past eight she could wait no longer. Forcing herself to stay calm, she dialled the Kenilworth number, and then all she had rehearsed went out of her head, for Maggie had answered the phone and Georgina heard herself babbling about this wonderful thing that had happened to her. How Tallis, her boss, had asked her to marry him, her words rushing one after the other as Maggie referred to their conversation of little more than a week ago when they had discussed marriage and how Georgina hadn't said a thing about being in love then.

'Oh, you know how it is, Maggie. I knew you were worried about me. I didn't want you to be further worried by knowing I was in love with no hope then, as I thought, of my love being returned. You may remember that I told you I was single because the right man hadn't asked me to marry him yet—well, he has now, and ...'

'And,' Maggie butted in, the lightness in her tone telling Georgina she was believed, 'now that he has you're just bubbling over because you're so happy.'

Maggie then went on to say how happy she was for her too. Then Nicola wanted to speak to her and was squeaking with delight that she was going to have a stepbrother-in-law, and asking if she could be bridesmaid.

'We haven't set the date yet, darling,' she told Nicola, not liking to have to include Nicola in her deception, but knowing there was no other way. 'Er—is Josh there?'

She had suspected Josh would be the most difficult of all to convince, and he was.

'A bit sudden, isn't it?' he asked, and she could almost hear his brain ticking over.

'Yes, it is,' she agreed, ready with part of what she had rehearsed. 'And I have you to thank, Josh, for making it all happen.'

'Me!' Josh exclaimed, but sounding interested.

'Yes, you,' she said, and went on to explain, 'Just before you came to the office last Friday I'd been working with my tape machine.'

'Yes, I saw you switch it off,' said Josh, to her great delight.

'That's the whole lovely part of it, Josh. I didn't switch it off—oh, I thought I had, but I'd switched to record instead, and our whole conversation, that bit about me telling you that the man I loved didn't know I existed, went on tape. Tallis had played it back by the time I returned to the office, and he asked me about it. And oh, Josh, isn't it wonderful, one thing led to another and he told me he felt the same way about me!'

She held her breath as she waited for Josh to speak, and let her breath out on a sigh of relief that he sounded as happy for her as Maggie and Nicola had done when he said:

'I'm very pleased for you, Georgie.'

'Er—that isn't all,' she said, knowing she was going to have to go very carefully from now on. Just one slip and it could all go for nothing. 'When Tallis and I got round to talking of other things, he wanted to know what all that was about you leaving school. He thought it was very manly of you, Josh, but he told me that when we're married my personal allowance will be more than twice my present salary.' Then she was gabbling again. 'Don't you see, Josh? It would be ridiculous for you to leave school. There'll be absolutely no need.'

She thought there was fresh hope in his voice as he told her he did see, and her heart swelled with love for him and unbounded gratitude for Tallis, for all Josh asked wouldn't Tallis mind her sending money home to them.

'Of course he won't. He's a wealthy man, Josh, and above everything else he wants me to be happy.'

The next question Josh asked was unexpected, and had her speaking off the top of her head. And when she eventually put down the phone, there was a stunned look about her. Had she really committed Tallis to going to Kenilworth with her for lunch on Sunday?

Happiness, for after lying for all she was worth, she had Josh's agreement that he would stay on at school, mingled with a sick feeling in the pit of her stomach at the magnitude of what she had done. The very last thing Tallis would want to do this Sunday would be to go with her and meet her family. But what else could she have done? Josh had been the one to ask the one question she hadn't thought of, but realised now she should have done.

'When are we going to meet him?' he had enquired. And she'd heard her own voice saying how Tallis was dying to meet them all. And then Maggie was back on the phone suggesting that they come to lunch on Sunday.

Her sick feeling deepened as she imagined the volley of sarcasm that would come rocketing her way when she told Tallis. How could she ask him to go with her? Yet everything would be ruined if he wouldn't. Oh, she'd put up with any amount of sarcasm if he would agree—but would he? And how could she ask him? She fell to wondering what he usually did with his Sundays. Naomi Garrick hadn't telephoned for over a week, but Georgina felt an added disquiet she couldn't understand when she imagined him spending his Sundays with women with sultry voices like that of Naomi Garrick.

Restlessly, she knew suddenly that she couldn't wait until tomorrow to confess what she had done, or to beg Tallis, if need be, to go with her on Sunday. She reached for the telephone directory, then her doorbell rang.

Perhaps it was because she was half dreading her caller might be Desmond and she had more than enough on her mind without having to tell him she couldn't see him, though he should be at his business dinner by now, or maybe it was because the person she really needed to talk with was Tallis, but when on going downstairs and pulling open the front door, she saw Tallis standing there, she could do nothing about the absolutely beaming smile that left her, or the heartfelt words that sprang to her lips.

'Oh, Tallis, I'm so glad it's you!'

For one second Tallis looked shaken by her greeting, and for another second it was Georgina who was shaken as it looked as though he was going to take her in his arms.

Then the hands that had seemed to move without thought from his sides dropped again, and he covered his action with a smile of his own and said pleasantly:

'What a welcome! I think I'm glad it's me too.' Then, his smile fading, 'Who else were you expecting?'

'Oh, no one,' Georgina said hurriedly, inviting him in and hoping he would remain as sweet-tempered when she told him what she had to tell him. 'I've messed things up a bit, I think.'

Tallis went with her up to her flat, and at her invitation sat down in the easy chair before taking her up on what she had said.

'How have you messed things up?' he asked. 'You've already phoned your people?'

'Yes,' Georgina said, and told him most of the conversation that had taken place, only found she just couldn't bring out the bit which would take care of a few of his Sunday leisure hours.

'You say Josh has agreed to stay on at school?' Tallis asked, as though trying to see where in all she had told him she had messed things up.

Knowing now was the time to come clean, she couldn't look at him as she said, 'Yes, that's right. Only—only—Josh asked when were the family going to meet you. And—well, I was so scared of ruining everything that when Maggie invited us to lunch on Sunday I—er—said we would go.' Dead silence greeted this piece of information, and she just had to look at him then to see how he was taking it. 'I'm sorry, Tal ...' she began, raising her head, and stopped right there, because Tallis wasn't giving her that dark frowning look of displeasure, but seemed, if anything, to be nodding in agreement.

He observed her anxiety for a moment, then said quietly, 'There's no call for you to be sorry, Georgina. It's perfectly natural that your family should want to see what sort of man you've got yourself engaged to.'

The word 'engaged' barely penetrated her mind as she stared at him in wonder. 'You mean you don't mind?—that you'll come with me? I thought . . .'

'Of course I'll come with you,' he shattered her by saying, then shattered her further by adding, 'As a matter of fact I'd planned to be with you when you made your call, thinking your family might think it odd that as a newly engaged woman you were spending the evening alone. But I got caught in a traffic snarl-up.' Then as Georgina just sat and wondered at his thinking, he said, 'I skipped my coffee to get here, as I thought, in time. Are you going to be a loving fiancée and make me a cup?'

She liked him in this teasing mood, she thought, as she busied herself in the kitchen. And she found herself liking him even more when, their coffee drunk, he stayed chatting with her, drawing her out to tell him about her home in Kenilworth. She was unaware that the affection she felt for her three step-relations was showing in her face as she told him about each one of them in turn.

'There's love as well as loyalty in you for them, isn't there?' he observed.

She smiled at him. 'It would be impossible not to love them,' she said simply. 'Maggie has always been so good to me, and Josh and Nicola—well, we love each other as if we were real brother and sisters.'

The minutes flew by with no disharmony showing itself. Then just when she was thinking how nice Tallis was being, the phone rang. With the phone being on a small table next to the settee, privacy was out of the question. But just then Georgina was feeling so amicable towards Tallis that there wasn't a thing she would mind him overhearing.

Excusing herself, she stretched out a hand and lifted the

receiver, and as she heard Desmond's voice, wished with all her heart that she had an extension somewhere, for she knew she wasn't going to be able to keep the identity of her caller secret. Tallis was shrewd enough to guess, and should he be in doubt, then she well knew that he wasn't above asking.

Looking down at her lap, anywhere but at him, she told Desmond she had thought he would be in the middle of his dinner by now.

'I told you I was expected to take a partner,' Desmond reminded her, sounding particularly blue. 'I didn't feel like going on my own. Have you been in long?'

About to say a couple of hours, she suddenly remembered she had told him she would be working late. 'Not long,' she answered, wanting above all else to finish the call, because Tallis was being very still, and she just knew he had discerned who her caller was, and since it must be obvious to him that she hadn't told Desmond she wouldn't be seeing him again, she knew he expected her to do so now. Only she couldn't, not with Desmond sounding so fed up with himself.

'Would it be all right if I came round for half an hour?' Desmond asked, a question she thought was perfectly acceptable between friends when one of them was fed up with their own company.

'I'm—I'm sorry, Desmond,' she replied, and couldn't help the lack of regret in her voice, though she did regret his name had tripped off her tongue, giving Tallis confirmation she was sure he didn't need as to the identity of her caller. 'I've got someone with me, actually.'

'Oh,' said Desmond. 'Anyone I know?'

'Er—Tallis.' No point in hedging.

'He brought you home from the office, did he?'

'We've just been having coffee,' Georgina said, which

she hoped would pass as an answer to his question. Then her ears picked up a sound that told her Tallis was growing impatient, and she knew she had better finish her call quickly, because it wouldn't surprise her in the least if Tallis came and snatched the phone out of her hand and said something short, sharp and concise to Desmond, or alternatively, slammed the phone down.

But fortunately at that point Desmond seemed to get the idea that she wasn't easy talking to him with Tallis there, and it was he who terminated the conversation with an, 'I'll give you a ring in the week.'

The harmony that had been in the room before the phone rang was a thing of the past after Desmond had rung off. Georgina felt tension in the air even before she glanced up and saw Tallis standing looking hard-eyed and stern-faced.

'I thought we agreed you weren't seeing Warner again?'

'I'm not seeing him again.'

'You've not told him yet, though, have you?'

Georgina looked at those hard eyes and knew he would never understand her reluctance to do so, or why. 'I will,' she said.

'Make damn sure you do. If I hear you've so much as *accidentally* bumped into him, then the agreement between us is at an end, and your job with it.' The words were barked at her with not a hint that he had a more gentle side to his nature.

'I've said I'll tell him,' she reiterated, panic within her. She knew he meant every word. He looked at her for long un-smiling seconds, then strode towards the door. 'I'll let you out,' said Georgina, ever mindful of the tendency of the front door to bang and shake the house.

Tallis stopped in his stride, and having started to move Georgina came to a halt beside him. 'You always make a point of seeing your—men friends off the premises?' he queried, his reference to the time he had observed her seeing Desmond out barely veiled.

About to explain about the front door, she saw that wasn't the point Tallis was making, and a spurt of anger had her saying sarcastically:

'Sometimes that chore is more pleasant than at others,' and she knew from the way his eyes had narrowed, the hard look changing to flint, that he had gleaned from that that she hated to see Desmond go, but that she just couldn't wait to be rid of him.

Then suddenly her anger was fleeing, and in its place came a little spasm of fear. For so quick did Tallis move, she just didn't have time to back away as her upper arms were gripped in an unbreakable hold and she felt herself being hauled up against his hard frame.

'I really have got myself a sweet little fiancée, haven't I?' he said grittily. 'I wonder if the traditional sealing of our bargain will take some of the sourness out of you.'

'Let me go, Tallis,' Georgina said stonily, giving a mighty wrench that proved ineffectual. 'You know I'm not your proper fiancée.'

'Admitting at last to being *im*proper, Georgina?' Tallis jibed, his head coming nearer to her own and making her insides turn over madly.

'I'm admitting nothing,' she said, trying to pull her head back out of range, only to find Tallis was quite capable of holding her still with one arm that was an iron band around her, while placing her head in the direction he wanted it with his free hand. Then before she could do anything about it, his mouth was closing over hers, and she was experiencing again that madness that had assailed her the first time he had kissed her.

Tallis wasn't satisfied with just one kiss, and after the

briefest of moments when his lips left hers and Georgina
was thinking this was insane and she had better do something quickly because she didn't trust herself any longer,
not with him, he again took her mouth, and then, insane or
not, she could do nothing to stop her lips from parting beneath his, and he no longer had to forcibly hold her to
him, because she was yielding, yielding, yielding.

Her arms went up and around him. She felt the con-
vulsive movement of him as it registered that her resistance to him had gone. And then she wasn't thinking any
more, but just living for each wonderful new sensation he
was arousing in her. Effortlessly he had her shirt separated
from her jeans, she felt his warm touch at the skin of her
back going higher and becoming more intimate, and she
felt no shame in the knowledge that she wanted him. There
couldn't be any shame, could there, because being in his
arms, glorying in his touch, knowing he wanted her as
much as she wanted him, she knew at that moment exactly
why Tallis had the power to upset her the way he so constantly did. She was in love with him.

Drowning in his touch, completely oblivious that he had
undone some of the buttons on her shirt to allow him to
slide her shirt over her shoulders, some part of her basic
inner reserve came to the surface just as Tallis was trailing
kisses over her shoulders. And as his fingers made to slip
her bra straps to one side, so a mocking inner voice reminded her that she wasn't the woman of the world he
thought she was.

Her arms dropped away from him. 'No,' she said huskily
to the dark head that was giving and taking pleasure from
her arched throat. She wanted to tell him why but couldn't.
Wanted to say, I don't really mean no, and explain, but
couldn't bear that he should laugh at her, and so she just

stood still, unsure in his arms, hoping yet dreading that he would completely ignore that negative word.

Aware she was no longer participating, but was standing unmoving in his arms, Tallis lifted his head, his eyes desire filled, taking in her flushed face. Then what she didn't want to see in his face was growing there—the warm look being ousted by frost as he controlled his quickened breathing. His arms falling away from her, and his voice when it came stiff with the restraint he was exerting.

'Lady,' he said, and took another deep breath before he continued. 'Lady, it might be as well another time to remember your manners—it just isn't polite to say yes physically, and then say no verbally.'

So he wasn't going to press her, Georgina thought, and wished that her microcosm of relief wasn't topped by screaming disappointment at the thought. And he was so right too. He knew full well there had been no physical resistance to him. Never having been in this position before, she just couldn't think of one single thing she could say.

'Why?' Tallis asked, taking a step away from her as though not quite trusting himself to heed her refusal.

'Why?' Georgina repeated, feeling gauche, idiotic and trying to remind herself she was twenty-six, for goodness' sake. 'Because it—er—doesn't—er—seem right.' She groaned inwardly—oh, God, she was sounding like a seventeen-year-old on her first date. She saw Tallis's right eyebrow ascend, and thought he was thinking the same too, a seventeen-year-old who had never been touched before. It was no help at all that at that moment something in her chemistry brought a blush to her skin.

But when Tallis spoke, she saw she had mistaken his thinking and her blush faded, only to rise again, this time in anger as he left her in no doubt the construction he had put on her words that it didn't seem right.

'Perhaps you're right,' he said, turning towards the door. 'I told you to get rid of Warner. Had you done so, your conscience wouldn't have reared its head at such an inauspicious moment.' He turned again, the door handle beneath his fingers. 'Perhaps it would be as well to shake off the old lover before you take on the new.'

Georgina was still gasping as he went through the door. The downstairs had crashed noisily too, before she had moved.

Having spent most of the night wondering how she could possibly be in love with a man who could be so insulting to her, Georgina just didn't know how she was going to face him the next day. But she discovered she had worked herself up unnecessarily, for his short, 'Good morning,' followed by him telling her he had put his dictation on tape and would be out most of the day, told her he had no time for anything that wasn't to do with work.

It was strictly business with him that day, with the next three days following the same pattern. And if she wondered that the man who had wrought havoc on her senses could treat her as though he had never taken her in his arms, as though he had never for an instant desired her, then she was very quick to adopt the same attitude. Never was he going to suspect she was in love with him.

It was Friday afternoon before any mention had been made of their engagement. As the day had worn on she had begun to be anxious. She didn't want to be the one to bring it up, but she was beginning to think he had forgotten all about it. Oh, but he couldn't, she thought worriedly. If he didn't go with her to Kenilworth on Sunday she just knew she would have her work cut out with Josh.

Tallis was late coming back from lunch, but when he did come in at half past three it was to stop by her desk, a hand casually in one of his pockets. Georgina lifted her head from her work, trying to give the impression that she hadn't been aware of him from the moment the door had opened. He had a meeting to go to shortly, and she knew she was just going to have to remind him about Sunday.

'About Sunday,' he said, his eyes flicking over her. 'I'll pick you up about ten.'

So great was her relief she couldn't stop the words from tumbling from her lips, 'I thought you'd forgotten,' and received a mocking look for her trouble.

'There's nothing connected with you, Georgina, that I forget,' he informed her, then pulling his hand out of his pocket, he placed a small square box on her desk. 'Make sure you wear that,' he said. And before she could get any of her thoughts together, he had gone into his office, collected his briefcase, was back and throwing over his shoulder as he went out a laconic, 'See you on Sunday.'

As engagement rings went, the sapphire and diamond ring Tallis had dropped so casually on her desk was sheer beauty. Having guessed what the box had contained, she had been absolutely speechless. That he should think an engagement ring would add more credence to their mock engagement, and that to cement that credulity he had handed over such an obviously expensive item, did nothing to lessen the love she had for him.

She was ready and waiting when Tallis called for her on Sunday. She had the engagement ring on her finger, had spent a full five minutes fantasising after she had put it on in looking at it and yearning to be the woman he loved.

Tallis glanced at her left hand before driving off, but he didn't appear to be any more talkative now than he had been since Monday, and her spirits dipped. If the hours in Kenilworth were to be spent with him in no mind to talk to her, then even surface-thinking Nicola wasn't going to be deceived into believing they were in love.

'How much does your stepmother know about Warner?' Tallis broke in on her thoughts.

Realising he was thinking Maggie might be suspicious of her sudden change of heart if she had already told her she was in love with Desmond, but having thought over the last few days that with Tallis thinking her in love with Desmond, it was a perfect screen for the love she had for him, Georgina limited her reply to:

'Maggie believes Desmond and I are friends, nothing more.'

Straightaway from the tightening of his expression she could tell he was thinking she was so far gone in her affair that she didn't care who she lied to, and her spirits dipped further at that tight look. She knew she was going to have to do something, say something, for if this was the way he was going to be with her in front of her family, then they might just as well turn round now and head back for London.

'Tallis,' she said, and then, the words coming quickly, 'you will try to pretend you're—you're in love with me, won't you?' Knowing her face had gone pink, she added equally quickly, 'When we get to Kenilworth, I mean.' She paused, only to gabble on, 'It's—it's so important that my family have no doubts when we've left this afternoon.'

For long seconds Tallis said nothing, then quietly he asked, 'Are you going to try to pretend you're in love with me?'

Georgina knew she didn't have to try. There would be no pretence about it. 'Yes,' she answered, her throat feeling choked.

'Then relax,' she was told. 'I'm not likely to drool over

you every other minute, but I think I can act the loving fiancé.'

Their greeting in Kenilworth was as warm and as happy as Georgina had thought it would be. And it was after lunch, with the five of them sitting back having coffee with no one in a hurry to leave the table, that she had the chance to look in turn at the four people she loved most in the world. Maggie had taken to Tallis immediately, Josh was more reserved but at ease with Tallis who addressed him on a man-to-man basis, Nicola was already looking half way to becoming besotted with him, making Georgina think that Leo Sayer had better look to his laurels, and lastly Georgina looked at Tallis, and her love for him knew no bounds. He had said he would act the loving fiancé, and he had done so—so much so, she had begun to feel herself loved, had several times had to rapidly bring herself back to reality, to remind herself that this was just a game they were playing and that she could so easily give herself away if she reciprocated too fully.

Not that Tallis had been obvious in his act to make it look as though he loved her. It was just the little things— the hand lightly brushing her honey blonde hair as if he couldn't stop himself when he had pulled out her chair for her, the way he had looked at her a second longer than necessary as though he couldn't bear to look away.

Not wanting to drag her eyes away from him, all male in his well-fitting fine check suit and pale green shirt, she realised she had been looking at him for far too long, and while he was safely in conversation with Josh, he could easily turn his eyes in her direction. Georgina pulled her love-filled eyes away from him, only to find Maggie had been looking at her. And then Maggie smiled, a gently warm smile, and Georgina knew in that instant that Maggie knew her secret. Maggie knew she was in love with Tallis.

They both turned their heads in Nicola's direction on hearing her saying to Tallis, 'It's a good job you're Georgie's boss, isn't it?'

'I'll agree with you there,' said Tallis. 'But why particularly, Nicola?'

Nicola, who had never been shy, suddenly went a shade pink at having all Tallis's attention on herself. 'Well,' she said, her eyes flickering to her stepsister, 'we forgot to put the clocks forward the last time Georgie was home and Georgie had to catch a later train. If you hadn't been her boss she would have got into trouble, wouldn't she?'

Not by so much as a flicker of an eyelash did Tallis reveal what he thought of this explanation he had never given Georgina the chance to reveal for her being late, or the fact that her returning by train endorsed that wherever Desmond Warner had gone that weekend, it had certainly not been with Georgina, since had that been so they would certainly have driven back in Desmond's car.

Once the washing up was out of the way and Maggie's invitation that they stay for tea gently refused by Georgina, Nicola asked if they had time for a walk before they went back.

'Why not?' smiled Tallis, before Georgina could again invent some excuse, suspecting that, his duty done, that Tallis would want to get back to London.

Their walk took them across the common, and Georgina wasn't even sure how Tallis and Josh became detached from the small group, but after answering some query of Nicola's, she looked up to see Tallis and Josh some way in front, obviously deep in a discussion about something.

It took all her discipline not to chase after them and break up their conversation, afraid as she was that Tallis might unthinkingly say something that would give Josh food for thought when they had gone. And then quite suddenly her panicky feelings fled, and the conviction came over her that Tallis would watch every word he said to Josh; she could trust him, he would not let her down.

'You've tumbled badly, haven't you, love?' said Maggie by her side, who unbeknown to her had been watching her face.

Georgina found a light laugh. 'Is it so obvious?'

'Only to me, love,' Maggie said happily. 'I know you better than most. But don't be afraid to let Tallis see it, he loves you too.'

Oh, Maggie, Georgina thought. Oh, Maggie!

On their way back, at the house, Nicola looked at Tallis's sleek car standing outside and reminded Georgina of the rather over-large picture belonging to her that hung in her old bedroom, and which countless times she had said she would take with her the next time, but had never done so because of the difficulties in carrying it.

'You could take it with you today,' said Nicola.

Tallis had no objection to transporting her picture, and once it was reposing in the back of his car it was time for them to be on their way.

'I'll write,' said Georgina, as she did every time she left them, then was being hugged by her family, even Josh, before getting into the car.

Kenilworth had been left behind when she turned to Tallis to give him her unhesitating thanks, telling him that everything had gone much better than she had dared to hope.

'No prick of conscience at the deception?' he asked.

'Of course,' she said, more sharply than she had meant, but what did he think she was, for goodness' sake? 'But you must see the deception was necessary. Josh has to have his chance. He's so bright it would be criminal for him not to have the future he's set his heart on—criminal to let his brain go to waste,' she added, having thought that after having seen Josh for himself, she wouldn't have needed to explain all this. Tallis remained silent and she found herself searching for other instances of Josh's analytical mind with which to impress on him how bright her stepbrother was. 'Maggie never discussed her finances with him,' she told him, 'but even so, he worked out that even with a grant it would be a struggle to keep him at university.'

'And that's where you come in, isn't it? You intend that he will want for nothing while he's studying,' Tallis inserted, the light note in his voice telling her she wasn't getting through to him. 'There'll be other things he'll need besides books and equipment.'

He had no need to tell her that already Josh's clothes were man-sized, and he had to have some social life too. But she had planned for that. She wasn't having him losing his youth solely to his studies.

'He'll have everything he needs,' she said with some determination.

'I don't doubt it,' said Tallis with equal conviction, she thought, and she remembered seeing the two of them deep in conversation and wondered if Tallis had seen from his talk with Josh how important it was that he had his chance. She hesitated to pry into what they had been talking about, but knew Tallis wouldn't tell her without her prompting him, not then either if he didn't feel like it.

'Er . . .' she began, looking for a delicate way to poke her nose in, and not finding one, but since he was waiting for her to continue, asking outright, 'What were you and Josh talking about?' and blushing for her sins.

'My, what a long nose we've got!' said Tallis, which relieved her blush that there was a teasing note in his voice, though what he had to tell her had her eyes going bigger and bigger as he proceeded to satisfy her curiosity. 'You'd already told me about his keen mind, and from the odd scraps of conversation we had at lunch that was borne out. But I wanted to find out for myself what sort of potential he has.'

'So you deliberately got him on his own so you could assess for yourself the alertness of his mind—how far along he is with his studies?' she asked, not sure she was very happy that Tallis had taken it on himself to do so.

But Tallis admitted it as though he could see no wrong in what he had done, then turned his head to glance at the unsmiling face turned to him. Then he grinned at her, that grin that had her forgiving him anything as her heart started dancing the samba.

'You'd told me about his gifted brain, but if you'll forgive me, Georgina, for thinking your opinion, because of your affection for him, might not be impartial.' She had to take that as fair comment, but was about to quote Josh's school reports as a back-up to her own opinion when Tallis said, 'I agree with everything you've said of him—he should have a very bright future ahead of him.' Then Tallis said something that had her staring at him open-mouthed. 'I agree it would be criminal for him not to have his chance. That's why I've decided that Chestertons will award him a medical scholarship.'

'Scholarship?' Georgina croaked, hardly able to take in what Tallis was telling her, so thunderstruck was she. 'B-but Chestertons only a-award engineering scholarships,' she heard herself protesting.

'Then it's about time we branched out a bit,' he said, and when, her thoughts clearing, she belatedly went to thank him, he asked her if she could leave him to concentrate as there was a tricky part of road coming up.

Left to herself, Georgina had to battle with not only her thoughts but with tears that wanted to spill over. Tallis was

proving himself more and more endearing with every breath
he took.

That opinion dipped slightly when after carrying her
picture up to her flat, he refused her offer of tea, saying he
had an appointment. But even though jealousy was gnawing away at her as her mind took off to wonder who that
appointment was with, she just couldn't let him go without thanking him for what, through him, Chestertons were
going to do for Josh.

'Thank you for coming with me today, Tallis,' she said
softly, then her voice grew husky as she looked at the man
who was less than a step away from her in her small flat.
'And thank you a million times for what you're doing for
Josh.'

What came over her then, she agonised for hours after
later. But with Tallis standing so close, not looking unapproachable as he had so many times in the past, her love
and gratitude to him at that moment rose up and swamped
her, and without thinking, she took a small step, then
leaned up and kissed his mouth.

Shock at what she was doing hit her the instant she
made contact with his warm lips. But shock or no, as she
felt a minuscule movement of his lips against hers, she
just couldn't pull away. Then Tallis's mouth was still and
hard hands were pushing her away, and night-black eyes
were fixing her with a fiery look, and he was ripping into
her:

'Stop right there! We both know the instant our lovemaking threatens to go all the way Warner will make himself felt in your mind. But I'm warning you now, the next
time you do that I shan't stop until I've erased him completely from your thoughts, so just don't start anything
you don't want me to finish—there'll be no turning back
the next time.'

Georgina was definitely jittery as she made her way into the Chesterton building the next morning. What had possessed her to kiss Tallis? Oh, her gratitude to him for what he was going to do for Josh was endless, but was she so little in control of herself that everything she had always believed herself to be counted for nothing when she was in the same room alone with him?

Knowing her impulses had to be repressed, determined that today and from now on not once was she going to say or do anything that took their relationship away from a business level, she pushed open her office door.

'Good morning, Georgina.' Tallis, as was his custom most mornings, was there before her, and straightaway she felt all her stern lectures of last night on how she would be with him the next time she saw him take a severe slide, for his voice held none of the animosity she was expecting.

'Good morning, Tallis,' she answered with a coolness she couldn't help feeling proud of. If she could keep it up, who knew, eventually she might even get a decent night's sleep, for whenever she let herself go with him it seemed she always spent the ensuing night in taking apart every word, every look, that had passed between them.

With a glad feeling that at least Tallis hadn't started the day off by barking at her, she bent down to stow her handbag away, and straightened up to see he had left his office and had come to stand by her desk. She saw his eyes go to her ringless left hand, then whatever he had come in to tell her was lost, as was any pleasantness he had found to greet her with.

'Where's your ring?' he snapped, his brow looking set for thunder.

'In my bag,' she said, having meant to return it him this morning, and bent to retrieve her bag so she could do so now.

'Put it on,' he ordered.

'Put it on?' she questioned. 'I thought ...'

'Put it on now,' he commanded shortly, obviously not at all interested in what she thought. 'I didn't get myself tied up to you just for the sheer hell of it.'

Georgina's eyes sparked as much from his tone as from finding that he thought her some booby prize he had been landed with. But before she could speak and send all her resolutions scurrying for the nearest drain, he was letting her know, in case she had forgotten, that their engagement wasn't solely for her benefit.

'I'm expecting Edgar Rankin in a few minutes, so get that ring on fast, and for God's sake stop looking as though you'd like to use my head as a punchball!'

Having given his orders, without waiting to see if she had complied, he stormed back to his room, the door closing between them, none too politely, she thought from the crash of it.

Shortly afterwards the outer door opened, and though still fuming against Tallis, Georgina had managed to retrieve some of her calm—sufficient anyway to reply graciously to Edgar Rankin's offered, 'Good morning.'

She was busy typing when Tallis escorted his uncle back through her office, but stopped when Tallis came and laid an arm lightly about her shoulders.

'I've just been telling Edgar our news, darling,' he said, and sourly she gave Tallis full marks for being such a brilliant actor that he managed to make it sound as though he thought himself favoured by the gods at his good fortune, for all just the touch of his arm across her shoulders was making her wilt.

'I'm sure you'll both be very happy,' said Edgar Rankin, bringing out his best manner in the circumstances, she thought as she watched his eyes go to her engagement ring.

'It's a pity you have to go away at this precise moment, Tallis, but that's the way it goes.'

Georgina managed to keep her face fairly impassive at the news that Tallis was going away, and wondered if that was what he had originally come in to tell her before he had noticed her bare hand. Edgar Rankin didn't stay very long, but by the time he went, Tallis had taken his arm from about her.

'You're going away?' she asked calmly, feeling strangely awkward now they were alone.

'A crisis has developed with our overseas division,' he informed her, moving to the front of her desk where he could see her front face. 'Our representative flew in from the States last night, and after I'd read through the documents he brought me, I could see there's nothing for it but for me to go over.'

He'd been working last night! He hadn't left her yesterday for some Naomi Garrick type, then, she thought, feeling inordinately pleased about that. 'When—are you going?' she asked, when what she wanted to ask was, 'When will you be back?' He hadn't gone yet and already she was feeling bereft. And she'd thought of looking for another job! How could she bear not to see him again, yet this position was only temporary until Mrs Fry was recovered, she must remember that.

'I'll be flying out tomorrow. Can you work late tonight?' Georgina only just managed to keep her eyebrows level that he was actually *asking*, not ordering. 'I've a lot to get through,' he said, and gave her a smile of such charm that her backbone threatened to melt. 'Your help will be invaluable.'

'Of course,' she replied, holding on firmly. One more smile like that and she'd be on her knees!

The next hour flashed by with Georgina making rapid

notes as Tallis instructed her what to do in his absence,
which would stretch into three weeks. Popping back into
her office to look for a mislaid file they needed, she looked
up from her pending tray to see him coming towards her,
the missing file in his hands. The interruption of the telephone broke into anything either of them would have said,
but she smiled at him, a deluge of warmth flooding through
her that they were working so well together. And then all
the warmth in her fled, and she was once more on thorns.
For her caller was Desmond, and with Tallis standing
barely a yard away, she couldn't hope to hide that her call
was personal, and who else rang her at work but Desmond?

'Lara has just been on—she tells me you're engaged to
Tallis,' he began promptly, his voice sounding somewhat
incredulous as he asked if there was any truth in it. Edgar
Rankin hadn't wasted any time, had he?

'Er—yes,' she said, and wished Tallis would go into his
own office and close the door behind him. But the glance
she flicked at him, his face unsmiling, told her he had no
intention of going anywhere. She turned her attention
back to Desmond, trying to inject a happily ecstatic note in
her voice—it was uphill work. 'Tallis and I are engaged,'
she confirmed lightly, and found any enthusiasm she could
inject at her good fortune was not welcomed, for Desmond
was sounding hurt that she hadn't wanted him to be the
first to know, and she realised then that he was having one
of his down days. Or was it that Lara had taken the opportunity to have another stab at him? Whatever the reason
for his depression, she could do little to get him out of it
with Tallis picking up every word.

'I had no idea you were even interested in him,' Desmond
was going on, saving the need for her to say anything.
'Though I suppose I should have twigged that you were
interested in him when you told me he was there in your

flat the night I phoned.' From that she gathered that he had cottoned on that few men were ever invited inside her flat. Then he was sounding more dejected than ever as he asked, 'Does this mean you won't be going out with me again?'

'I ...' All too conscious of Tallis's eyes boring into her, she knew that two men were waiting for her to deliver the lines that would sever her friendship with Desmond. 'Well,' she said, bracing herself against the loneliness she was going to hear in his voice, 'I'm afraid so, Desmond.' His name came out gently, and by then she was past caring that Tallis heard it—he knew who she was speaking with, anyway.

She heard a resigned sigh come from the other end of the phone, followed by, 'It's going to be lonely without you, Georgina, but,' as if he was fighting his depression, and that upset her too, 'Tallis isn't a man to stand for you being friends with another man, is he, even if that friendship is only platonic. Be happy, Georgina, you deserve the best.'

Her eyes were moist when she put the phone down. That note in Desmond's voice as he tried to beat his depression had her vividly recalling her father's depression when her mother had left them, and she felt she had sorely let him down. She became aware of an irritated sound behind her, an exploded oath, she thought, followed by, 'For God's sake!' and lifted her saddened face to be pinned by a look from Tallis that told her his temper was on the shortest fuse to date. Then as if he didn't trust himself to speak to her, he thrust the file he was holding at her, and slammed out.

It was sheer pride and stubbornness that got her through the rest of that day. Tallis had returned shortly after he had stormed out, and was, in a word, unbearable.

By the time it came to seven o'clock, her spirits were bruised and aching. Many times during the rest of that day it was on the tip of her tongue to reveal everything there was to know of her friendship with Desmond, her fears for his mental health, and the loneliness of spirit he carried with him. But each time the impulse came, one look at Tallis's unapproachable expression and the impulse died.

The last note taken, Georgina covered her typewriter and made to depart, her rock bottom spirits not helped by the thought that she had no idea when she would see Tallis again. He hadn't offered to feed her as he had the last time she had worked late, she would have refused anyway; there seemed no point of communication between them and she knew he couldn't wait to see the last of her.

'I'll most likely see you when you get back,' she said, aiming for an uncaring tone.

'I'll see you home.'

'There's no need.'

'Get your coat,' he ordered in a tone that ended all argument.

The journey to her flat was completed in silence, during which time Georgina bottled down her feelings and sought for some suitable parting remark for when the car stopped.

An inate courtesy in Tallis, she thought, had him getting out of the car and standing on the pavement outside her apartment, but he made no move to go any further.

'H-have a good flight,' Georgina bade him, and turned to go, only to find her arm caught as he turned her back to him, his fingers gripping hard, his expression granite as he looked down at her.

'Just remember you're engaged to me,' he told her in no uncertain terms. 'Remember exactly *why* you're engaged to me. And remember, when the feelings you have for my cousin's husband get on top of you, that if you see him just once, then the future you want for your stepbrother won't even get off the ground.' With that Tallis threw her arm away from him and strode back to his car. It was roaring away before she had the front door closed.

Once inside her flat, all the tension of her pent-up feelings broke, and Georgina sat down and cried and cried until she could cry no more. When she had no more tears left, she went into the bathroom and sluiced her face, wished that she could hate Tallis, and found she still had a reserve of tears as more began to flow.

CHAPTER NINE

HEAVY-EYED but much calmer the next morning, Georgina was able to think of Tallis without giving way to tears, and recalling his parting words knew that if she had anything to do with Desmond, not only would Josh not get his scholarship, but she would be out of a job. Well, she certainly wasn't going to do anything to spoil Josh's chances, and anyway Desmond had accepted yesterday that the companionable evenings they had shared were a thing of the past. No, she wouldn't be hearing from Desmond again.

But she discovered she was wrong there. Tallis had been gone two days when, as she was feeling a restlessness, a loneliness of spirit, the phone in her flat rang, and it was Desmond, sounding as lonely as she was feeling.

'I heard Tallis was in the States,' he said. 'I thought you might be lonely for the sound of another voice.'

After that call, Desmond rang her many times. It was always just after nine, as though the long evenings had to be broken by communication with someone. Often Georgina made up her mind to tell him not to ring again, but every time as they both relieved their loneliness, the call would end with her never having done so, and each time she consoled her conscience by thinking, well, she wasn't actually *seeing* him, was she?

When Tallis had been away for two weeks, Georgina, heart-sore for the sight of him, determined that with the time drawing nearer for his return, if Desmond rang tonight, then she would definitely tell him not to do so again. But when just after nine her phone rang and Desmond, who had been sounding much more cheerful, now sounded as though he had hit another bad patch, she just didn't have the heart to tell him. She would next time, she promised herself, she would next time.

She received a jolt the following day when Mrs Fry, looking blooming with health, popped into the office, and Georgina realised her temporary job might be over before she saw Tallis again.

Mrs Fry confirmed she was as well as she looked, but saved her asking the question that was burning her lips by adding, 'The doctor says I can return to work any time I like now,' and as Georgina's heart plummeted, 'but Mr York said when he came to see me that I wasn't to rush back.'

Georgina went home that night knowing it was possible to sink lower than rock bottom. Seeing Mrs Fry today had been a vivid reminder that her time at Chestertons was limited. Would Tallis ever think about her once she had returned to Partons? She held back tears as the answer came to her.

Thinking she was in for another long evening with thoughts of Tallis her main preoccupation, for all she was going to try and not think about him, she was taken out of the hopelessness of her thoughts when her door bell went.

Dressed in jeans and shirt, she went down the stairs as she was, hoping her bell had been rung in mistake for one of the other tenants; she didn't feel like making the effort to put on a cheerful face if the caller was for her.

Colour surged through every part of her body when pulling back the front door she saw the man who had occupied the majority of her thinking in the two weeks he had been away, and she was more than ever glad of the dim lighting so he couldn't see her raging colour, or the gladness in her eyes that just the sight of him brought. But she couldn't hope to hide that her voice was far from normal, when the exclamation broke from her:

'Tallis!' Then, control rushing in, 'What a surprise! I thought you were still in the States.'

'Are you going to invite me in?' His tones were even, giving her no idea why he had called, but she didn't care, it was enough just to see him.

'Of course,' she replied, stepping back, and even managed to keep up a cool sort of prattle as he went with her up the stairs.

Georgina's heart was foolishly singing as she invited him to sit down. She was fully aware it was ridiculous to be so glad to see him, but how wonderful to feel like this after being so low as to be submerged up to the second before she had opened the door to see him there.

Once they were both seated, this time with Tallis taking the settee and she taking the chair, he told her he had just flown in, but since his uncle would most likely ring him that night, he thought he would drop by to see if there was anything he should know about.

'No, everything's fine,' she told him, knowing he was referring to their engagement and thinking it was typical of Tallis not to be caught unarmed.

'You haven't seen anything of Warner while I've been

away?' he queried, looking ready to get uptight if her answer was in the positive.

Wishing she could be angry that he should feel the need to ask that question, she felt a blush of guilt at those telephone calls betray her, and remembering the time Desmond usually called her, her eyes flew to the clock. Oh dear, it was just after nine!

'Well?' Tallis demanded, taut aggression in every line of him. 'Have you been seeing him while my back has been turned?

If she had been truly engaged to him, he couldn't have looked more angry that he thought she had been playing him false, she thought, before she answered in a hurry when it looked as though he was going to get up from the settee and shake her till her teeth rattled.

'No. No, of course not,' she replied, and groaned inwardly, as right on cue the phone rang.

In a mind to let it ring, she saw that aggression was still with Tallis, and she didn't put it past him to answer the phone himself if she didn't do so. Going over to the telephone table near him, she kept her back turned as she lifted the receiver, knowing he was already aware she was guilty of something, and not daring to look at him. Praying it was Maggie, she heard Desmond's voice. Panic-stricken, she only waited to recognise his voice, then found herself gabbling, not wanting a long-drawn-out conversation:

'Tallis is here.'

To Desmond's credit, he caught on straight away that his call was most ill-timed. 'Sorry, Georgina, you want me to hang up?'

'Please.'

She replaced the receiver, sent up her biggest prayer yet in the hope that when she turned round she would find Tallis had gone. But on turning, she saw her prayer hadn't been answered. For he was still there—not sitting as he had been, but standing looking ready to annihilate her with words he wasn't going to be over-fussy about choosing.

'Has Warner rung you often while I've been away?' he gritted. And if she thought she had witnessed aggression in him before, it had been mild in comparison with him now as he towered over her.

'Yes,' she confessed, adding in a rush when it looked as though she might yet be physically shaken, 'H-He's lonely.'

'I'll bet he is,' Tallis said nastily. 'He hasn't had you warming his bed since we've been engaged, has he?'

'He never did have me warming his bed!' she snapped, temper coming, even with Tallis looking so downright murderous.

'Like hell he never did,' Tallis bit at her. 'You've responded to me like a normal full-blooded, passionate woman, so don't give me that "just good friends" bilge. Until your conscience pricked you about him, you showed me you welcome the ultimate in lovemaking.'

Georgina's temper fled, to be replaced by agonising disquiet. If she repeated that she hadn't slept with Desmond, then Tallis would know, since Desmond appeared to be the only man she went out with, that the response he had aroused in her wasn't usual. Barely thinking straight, riding high on emotions of that moment, neither Maggie, Nicola nor Josh figuring in her actions, she withdrew the ring she loved so much from her engagement finger.

'You'd better take this with you,' she said as calmly as she could, knowing she couldn't do anything else, and knowing too that she was going to howl her eyes out when Tallis had gone. She saw his jaw clench hard as he looked at the ring she was pushing towards him. Then his control snapped.

'Keep the bloody ring!' he bellowed, then, a thread of

control coming to him as he added through clenched teeth, 'And if you want your stepbrother to have that scholarship, you'll damn well wear it!'

How could she have put Josh's future in jeopardy? Georgina wondered as the house shook after Tallis had let himself out. And later in bed that night as she turned her head on her damp pillow, How could Tallis be so generous to her when by the very act of speaking to Desmond on the phone, she had given him sufficient cause to break their agreement?

By Friday Georgina felt she had had it with Tallis. She had thought he could be unbearable before he had stormed out of her flat, but in the days following he had proved that a bear with a sore head had nothing on him. Had Edgar Rankin chosen any moment during those days to drop by, then he couldn't but notice that it was taking Tallis all his time to be civil to her. And now, when as early as Monday she had been dreading Mrs Fry's return, she just couldn't wait for her to do so. Any ridiculous flights of fancy she had been idiotic enough to dream up, that because Tallis had shown he had briefly desired her he might yet come to like her a little, had been hammered out of her head by his manner with her since the night she had attempted to return his ring.

The aggression that must have had a hand in getting him to the top was about every inch of him this morning. He had a board meeting to chair in half an hour. Thank goodness it promised to last for the rest of the day. Georgina was growing weary of having to tiptoe round him rather than bring his wrath down on her head, for it seemed the slightest thing could trigger it off.

'Have you got those papers ready for me?'

She'd heard him come in, of course, was aware of every

sound made in that other room. It took her a minute or two to find the papers he wanted, which again was ridiculous because she had known he would want them and had put them where she could immediately find them.

Her face outwardly calm, though how she kept her fingers from trembling she didn't know, Georgina found the errant papers that Tallis was standing waiting none too patiently for.

'I think you'll find them in order,' she said quietly, and snatched her hand back when in handing the papers over, her fingers accidentally touched his.

'You've changed, Georgina,' said Tallis, his eyes like granite as they held hers, and as she waited for the jibe she was certain was to come, she wanted to cry that he could look at her with such cold dislike. 'There have been moments when the feel of my hands on you produced a very different reaction.'

The pig! The utter swine, she thought, keeping her face straight by some miracle, determined he shouldn't see her in tears.

'That was before I got to know how truly lovable you are,' she said with sweet sarcasm that came out of desperation not to let him see she was falling apart at the seams.

Those hard eyes glinted with a light that told her her sarcasm had hit home, and she drew back when Tallis made a movement as though to come towards her and prove he could still get the same response if he so wished. Then he checked, gave her one final look and departed for his meeting.

It was shortly after lunch that Georgina's seesawing thoughts had to give way to the priority of an unexpected nose-bleed. Preoccupied as she was with finding fresh tissue after fresh tissue, Tallis was forced out of her thoughts for a time. When her nose-bleed showed no signs of letting up, she went along to the first aid post, hoping for an instant cure.

There wasn't any instant cure. She was put to lie down for a while, but when each time she went to stand her nose began to bleed again, and since in an effort to oust Tallis from her thoughts she had put all her energies into her work and was now fairly clear, when it was suggested she had better go home, Georgina, having no wish to hear more of Tallis's ill temper should his meeting finish before five, decided to take the advice given.

'I have to go out in ten minutes,' said one of the assistants. 'I'll give you a lift home if you like.'

Gratefully Georgina accepted. Ten minutes would be all she needed to tidy her desk. Back in her office, her things put away, typewriter covered, she realised she'd better leave a message in case Tallis did come back.

Switching on the machine, she began to record, 'I've ...' then stopped on hearing her voice sounding all thick from the plugs that were to stay in her nose until she could get home to lie down. Tallis wouldn't be interested in her nose-bleed anyway, she thought, and decided to keep her message brief. 'I've gone home,' she said, sounding as though she had been crying non-stop for a fortnight, and signed off.

An hour's lie-down on her bed did the trick. There was no need to go along and see her doctor as the sick bay attendant had advised if her nose didn't stop bleeding. Tentatively Georgina got to her feet, walked slowly to the bathroom, not wanting to start anything up again, and decided, looking at her face in the bathroom mirror, that her face was not a pretty sight.

An hour later she was again inspecting her face. That was better! She had had a bath, dumped the clothes she had worn that day and now changed into well-fitting trousers and a shirt, felt much more like Georgina Underwood. Her nose still looked a little pink, she thought, and was of the opinion that though tissues were invaluable for casual use, frequent reference to them had the erosive quality of sandpaper.

The ringing of her door bell cut off further reflections, and checking her watch she saw it had just turned five. She couldn't help but think about Tallis as she went down to answer the door, purely she knew because he was never far from her thoughts, and the last time she had been summoned to the front door it had been Tallis. But it wouldn't be him this time, she thought, reaching the door. She didn't want it to be him in any case. It was enough to have to put up with his vile temper at work without having it following her home.

She pulled back the heavy front door and saw she was mistaken in thinking it wouldn't be Tallis. For there he stood, as big and as vital as ever, his face stern as he took in her face free of make-up and the pinkened tip of her nose.

Unspeaking, she stood back to let him in. It was as much a waste of time to close the door on that unsmiling face as to ask him on the doorstep what he wanted. Tallis would have no scruples about asking to come in and from what she could see he didn't look ready to argue the point should she refuse.

In silence they went up the stairs, but once inside her flat, Georgina had no intention of asking him to sit down. With luck he wouldn't be staying long.

'Warner has been in touch with you,' Tallis stated rather than asked once the door had been closed, and Georgina stifled a groan that he was back to Desmond, a sure sign they were going to fight.

'No, he hasn't,' she denied stonily.

'Lara, then?'

Lara! Why would Lara want to get in touch with her? 'The last time I spoke with Lara was when she phoned you at the office,' she said, hoping she could stay as cool-sounding until this interview was over. She wished Tallis would stop looking at her; he hadn't taken his eyes from her since she had turned and faced him.

'You've been crying,' he accused, and before she could deny it, 'You've heard the news from some other source.'

What news? she wondered, her heart, never very stable when Tallis was near, beginning to pump painfully that there was some news that was going to make her cry.

'I don't know what you're talking about,' she said, mystified, '. . . and I haven't been crying.'

Tallis continued to look at her steadily as though trying to see from her expression if she was telling the truth. 'Your voice on tape sounded as though you were upset,' he said.

Georgina's heart gave a little lift that he might have come straight round to see her because he thought she sounded upset, then it sank down again as she berated herself for being idiotic and ready to snatch at crumbs.

'I had a nose-bleed,' she explained. 'It wouldn't stop, so the first aid people plugged it so that I could come home to lie down.'

His eyes went to the pink tip of her nose, then lifted to hers. 'Then you don't know,' he said, some of his hardness leaving him. His voice was less sharp anyhow, she thought, as she realised that whatever the news was he thought she would cry over, he was going to have to be the one to tell her.

'Know what?' she asked, bracing herself for whatever it was.

'Shall we sit down?' he suggested.

Wanting now to know the news quickly, as it looked as

though he thought she was going to collapse as soon as she heard it, Georgina sat to one end of the settee only to find instead of taking the chair as she had thought, Tallis had come and sat down beside her.

'Edgar Rankin told me at the end of our meeting that Lara has gone back to Warner,' he said quietly, slewing round so he could observe her face.

'Lara's gone . . .' Georgina began, and tears did spring to her eyes—not because she was broken-hearted at this piece of news as he thought, but because she could just picture Desmond's unbounded joy.

She raised her shimmering eyes to him. 'How . . .' she began, meaning to ask how it had come about, but the look on Tallis's face stopped her from going any further. His face was stern, but there was such a look of gentleness in his eyes, tenderness almost, she thought, before she rejected such imaginings and labelled his look as one of sympathy for what he thought she was feeling at that moment.

'I believe Lara has wanted to go back to him for some time,' he told her. 'I remember once telling you I knew her very well, and I do. In my view she realised that while she's always been able to do most of what she likes with Warner, she came up against a stubbornness equal to her own when it came to getting him to close his business and come to Chestertons.'

Georgina had veiled her eyes when Tallis had begun to speak, but they flew open, startled, when she felt his hand come down to take hold of hers as it lay in her lap. That sympathetic look was still in his eyes, she saw, and she badly wanted to snatch her hand away but couldn't.

'You'll have to face it, Georgina,' Tallis told her quietly. 'Warner is in love with his wife.'

'You—you were saying you thought Lara has wanted to go back to him for some time,' she reminded him, trying to stay cool but feeling anything but while his thumb was absently caressing the back of her hand.

'Having made her stand, I believe it gradually began to dawn on her as the months went by that he wasn't going to back down. It wouldn't have been very much of a marriage had he done so,' he slotted in. 'Lara became desperate to find a way of getting back with him without having to lose face.'

'You're saying she found a way? That she's gone back to him without him having to give up his company?'

'That's what I'm saying,' he agreed, and his hand gripped hers tightly before he told her the way Lara had found. 'Hell, there's no way to dress this up,' he said, the first harsh note in the last five minutes making itself heard. And as she looked at him and waited, he sucked in a deep breath, then said shortly, 'Lara is pregnant.'

'Oh!' exclaimed Georgina in surprise, turning her face away. She didn't know why she was surprised, mainly she supposed, because she just hadn't thought of that possibility.

'Lara may be many things,' went on Tallis, who knew her well, 'but one thing she isn't, Georgina, and that is an adultress.'

So he wanted there to be no doubt when he left that she knew Lara's baby was Desmond's. Well, she hadn't thought otherwise. If Tallis expected her to break down and weep her heart out at that information, then he was unlucky, she thought, as he went on to make it even more clear.

'You do realise what I'm saying?' he asked gruffly. 'Lara hasn't broken the seventh Commandment. She's pregnant and . . .'

'And Desmond is the father,' Georgina inserted calmly. She was aware of Tallis's intent regard as though he couldn't understand that she was taking it so calmly.

'You realise,' he said slowly, 'that he couldn't have kept faith with you? That while you were still lovers he was ...'

'Sleeping with his wife? Yes, I knew that anyway. He told me ...'

'He *told* you!'

'Not in so many words,' Georgina said, hearing the incredulity in his voice that she had kept on with the affair he thought she was having while knowing Desmond was sleeping with his wife. 'But I did know.'

'And you didn't throw him over!' exclaimed Tallis, and she could see he was beginning to get rattled. Well, that was all right by her, because the fact that he thought she would hang around in such circumstances was getting her rattled too. The explosion she had thought was imminent wasn't very long in coming. 'What the hell sort of relationship did you have with him?' he almost shouted, his aggression becoming unleashed.

'I told you,' she said, inwardly trembling at the barely checked violence in him, but her pride exultant at the sweetness of her tone as she brought out, 'Desmond and I were friends.'

'Friends as well as lovers,' he hurled at her before she could draw another breath, his hand leaving hers. 'Well, I think I can safely say that your affair with him is at an end.' His temper had taken the sympathy she thought she had seen from him.

'Desmond and I were never lovers,' she said flatly, feeling worn down by his continued disbelief in anything she told him about her relationship with Desmond. It no longer seemed important that Desmond had once seemed a fine screen for her love for Tallis, since the only time she had been in danger of giving herself away had been when she had been in his arms, and from the way he was looking at her now, that was never likely to happen again.

'Why lie?' Tallis asked, as though growing tired of ever getting her to be honest with him. 'We both know you're in love with him. As much as you care for Josh, the moment I went abroad, you in essence broke our agreement by being unable to forget him and your need to have contact with him. And aside from that, if I needed more proof, there was a time when I held a warm, responsive woman in my arms...' His voice sharpened as he recalled the moment. 'You lapsed there, Georgina. You were all set to give yourself to me until you remembered him.'

That angry note was creeping back into his voice, but Georgina knew she just couldn't allow herself to rise to it. He was touching on a subject that spelt danger for her and she was only too well aware of it. Needing to draw him away from anything connected with that, she looked down at her lap, and her glance caught the beautiful sapphire and diamond ring. With Lara and Desmond back together again there was no need for Tallis to keep up his end of the charade, she realised, and not wanting to part with the ring, feeling as though she was breaking her last link with him, she withdrew it from her finger.

'You'd better take this,' she said. 'You won't have your uncle breathing down your neck any more, will you?'

If she had thought to get Tallis away from the subject of the way he could make her respond to him, then she soon saw as he ignored her outstretched hand, that if she didn't want to talk about it, then he did.

'You were all set to give yourself to me,' he repeated, and here his eyes narrowed as though he was doing some very thorough summing up. 'Was Warner the first?' he asked, his tone grim. 'Was he the one to take your virginity? Is it for that reason you feel yourself bound to him—that because of that there's no room for anyone else in your life?'

'No, he wasn't,' she snapped quite without thinking. Desmond hadn't taken her virginity, no one had, but she wasn't having sophisticated Tallis York roaring his head off if he found that out. Then the rest of what he had said started to clamour in her ears. 'No chance for anyone else?' she echoed. 'What do you mean?'

Hope flared briefly and she cursed that, so in love with him was she, she read her heart's desire in what he had said. Then as hope faded, anger began to grow in her and her temper flared, fanned by a let-down feeling at the folly of such hopes as it dawned on her that what Tallis might actually be saying was that he wanted her to forget Desmond so that he could take his place as her lover. Agreed, Tallis was the only man for her, but it hurt to the quick that what he was suggesting was an affair of—what—a month? Maybe two? No longer than it took for the desire she knew he had for her to be sated.

'If you're hinting that you'd like to take Desmond's place,' she said, trying to keep on top of her temper, 'then you can forget it.' She saw his face darken as her words hit him and knew his temper was coming to the boil and that any minute now they would be in the middle of a stand up fight.

'Damn you!' he snarled furiously. 'I don't want to take his place as your part-time lover, I ...'

'Well, it damn well sounded like it!' she burst in, refusing to be daunted that he looked mad enough to hit her.

'Can't your mind think past affairs?' he bit at her.

'*My mind!*' Astonishment had her gasping. 'It's you who's been constantly on about just that particular issue ever since I've known you.' All hold on her temper had gone and she just didn't care any more as she railed at him. 'You've never let a chance go by to have a dig at what you thought had been going on between Desmond and me!'

'You're still maintaining you were just good friends?' he growled at her, and she was past caring as his jaw jutted fiercely that they might yet come to blows. 'Good friends or not,' he said nastily, 'Warner had more than a friendly hold on you. You wanted me as I wanted you, yet he came between us, didn't he?'

Georgina sprang to her feet, too agitated to sit still any longer. He was like a terrier with a bone, and his persecution of her had her wildly out of control. He didn't seem ready to give up until he had stripped her soul bare.

'Desmond had nothing to do with that,' she said hotly, taking a pace away from him as Tallis stood up too and they faced each other, fury rife between them.

'Desmond had nothing to do with that,' he mimicked. 'Like hell he didn't!'

'He didn't!' Georgina yelled, unable to take much more, calm thinking a thing of the past. 'He's been terribly lonely waiting for Lara.'

'You knew she would go back to him?'

'No—it seemed most unlikely. I just hoped she would.'

She thought her reply had startled him, but he kept his surprise out of his voice as he said, 'Yet you were near to tears when I told you she'd done so.'

'Only because I was happy for him. I've thought just lately he was showing signs of strain, of mental exhaustion. I was afraid he might crack.'

The fury seemed to have died between them as suddenly as it had sprung up. Tallis was looking as though something was gnawing away at him, but at least he now appeared to be in a more reasonable frame of mind.

'So you're trying to tell me you only ever went out with him because of his loneliness?' There was a cynical, disbelieving note there, that had her temper on edge again.

'My father was lonely after my mother left us,' she told

him, not meaning to tell him anything of the sort, but finding herself going on, 'He was desperately lonely before Maggie and the children came to us. When I met Desmond last June ...'

'June!' Tallis interrupted her, his brow creasing in two lines, 'Lara left Warner last March.'

'I don't care what she told you,' Georgina said woodenly, 'she didn't leave Desmond because of me.'

She hadn't expected him to believe her, but thought she saw from his face that he knew his cousin well enough to know she could stretch the truth a little. He seemed to be giving her the benefit of the doubt anyway, as he said, 'Go on. You say you met Warner in June, and because of your remembrances of your father's loneliness you began going out with him.'

'I refused when he told me he was married,' she found herself confessing, and wanted to stop right there, but something was unlocking all these words from inside her. Maybe it was because Tallis wasn't yelling at her any more, but she couldn't seem to stop. 'But as you said, I remembered how lonely my father was, and since ...' She checked right there. Suddenly she knew she was telling him much too much.

'Since what, Georgina?' Tallis prompted, and completely unnerved her by putting out a hand and pulling her with him to make her sit down beside him on the settee. 'Since what?'

'Well, if you must know,' she said, agitation taking hold and adding to her disquiet at having Tallis so close, 'because of Josh, I'd decided I couldn't afford to have a permanent relationship—couldn't allow myself to fall in love because ...'

'But you fell in love with Warner!'

'No, I didn't!' she flared, then cooling rapidly and having to look anywhere but at Tallis, for her stormy denial seemed to be having the oddest effect on him as he was gripping her arm as though he never meant to let it go, 'I've known from the start that Desmond was in love with his wife. He only told her I was in love with him because she goaded him into it—he knew it wasn't true. You're hurting me!' she broke off to say as his grip tightened further, then she felt some relief when he took his hand away completely, though on looking down she saw his fists were tightly clenched as though he was having trouble with his self-control.

'Go on,' he urged again, when she had lost the thread of what she was saying. 'You said you knew Warner was in love with his wife.'

'Yes—well, with Desmond being in love with Lara, and his needing company, and with me not wanting to get tangled up with anyone until Nicola and Josh have finished their education, it turned into a nice safe friendship for us both.'

She looked at Tallis, but his set face was giving absolutely nothing away, and she just couldn't stop the sigh that escaped her, because it seemed to her that revealing all she had to him had been a waste of breath, for there was nothing in his face to say he believed her. And when next he began to speak, she just knew from his tone that he was highly sceptical of everything she had told him, and all she wanted then was for him to go and leave her in peace, knowing that the moment the door closed behind him she was going to call herself all sorts of a fool to have told him everything anyway.

'Would you mind telling me,' he asked levelly, 'what, if I'm to believe all you've told me—that you're not in love with him, that you've never been to bed with him,' the level note faded, 'then what in God's name was he doing saying goodbye to you in the early hours of the morning?'

Georgina swallowed, knew she would be wasting more breath, but striving for calm and hoping not to get rattled when Tallis said, as she was sure he would when she told him, 'A likely tale,' she said, 'Would you believe he'd left his briefcase in my flat before we'd gone out to dinner the previous evening. He wanted to make an early start the next morning, so he called to collect it.'

A tense silence followed her cool statement, but she was feeling far from cool as she waited to hear Tallis's scoffing laughter. She just couldn't look at him as she waited.

But Tallis didn't scoff. Nor did he laugh. And she wanted to cry as she heard the remorse in his voice as he said slowly, and very gently:

'I've been a cantankerous brute to you, Georgina, haven't I?'

At his words, tears did spring to her eyes making her keep her head averted so he shouldn't see. For, man of the world that he certainly was, she could only gather from that that he *did* believe her. But before she could clear her choked throat, before she could force humour into her voice and agree that he had been a cantankerous brute, Tallis was asking the one question it appeared he had never lost sight of.

'So with you and Warner only friends, what was it, then, Georgina, that had you holding back when it looked as though you were ready to give yourself to me?'

A warm pink stole over her skin. That was one question she just couldn't answer. Frantically she sought around in her mind for something that would change the subject, though she hardly thought Tallis would let her get away with it.

'Er—er—what were you doing driving past my door

that morning?' she asked, intent on keeping her head turned from him, only to find his fingers had come beneath her chin and her head was turned so he could see into her eyes.

'I didn't know myself then,' he told her, and those dark eyes of his seemed to be searching into her very soul as he refused to let her jerk out of his hold. 'I know now,' he continued solemnly, 'but at the time I convinced myself it was about time I had a change of scenery on my way to work.'

'But it *wasn't* just for the change of scenery?' she questioned, her voice becoming husky, for there was a warm look coming into his eyes as he looked back at her.

'No, my dear,' he said, and that 'my dear' had her heart pumping any way but the way it should. 'After our first meeting, for all I'd said I would be in touch with you again, I had no idea what made me say it, I had no such intention, or so I thought.' Here he allowed himself a small smile at her bemused face, but whether he knew he had her riveted attention, she couldn't tell. All she knew was that she wanted to hear more. 'Then that night at dinner I felt my interest in you growing.'

'You were interested in me?' she asked chokily, telling herself not to hope for anything because she had been fooled by hope before. Then common sense rushed in. 'Because you thought I was ruining Lara's chances of reconciliation?' she brought out flatly, and her heart began to pump erratically again as Tallis answered:

'I kidded myself that was the reason,' his other hand coming to take hold of hers in her lap. She swallowed as she waited. 'But the next day when I could easily have found myself another secretary from within the building, other secretaries just didn't figure.'

'Oh,' said Georgina. 'Er . . .' It was hopeless, she was just like some tongue-tied teenager, she could think of nothing to say.

'And then,' said Tallis, seeing she had nothing to add, 'when I was certain you were lying to me about your relationship with Warner, I found myself wanting to believe you so much that for a very short while I actually did.'

'Until you saw him leaving this house that morning,' she put in.

He nodded. 'If it's any consolation to you, Georgina, for the untrue things I've accused you of, for the vile way I've behaved with you this week——' Her eyes widened. 'Oh, I know I've been a perfect swine to you,' he said, 'but if it's any consolation to you, I've been through hell myself since I discovered what it is that's made me act the way I have done.'

His hands came from beneath her chin and stroked in a caressing whisper down the side of her face, and her thinking patterns went haywire.

'Y-you have?' she said, her voice high, unnatural, and not hers at all.

'I've been in hell with jealousy every time I've thought of you with Warner. Every time I've thought of you being in love with him my baser instincts have swept away all semblance of rational, civilised thinking.'

'But I'm not in love with him,' she said, having been fooled before in her imaginings, not daring to dwell on why Tallis had been so jealous of Desmond.

'I've accepted that, with much relief I may say, but—but,' and here, and this was something she had never imagined, for the worldly-wise, confident man she knew Tallis to be looked for once to be uncertain, unsure, and as though he couldn't be selecting his words more carefully if his life depended upon them, before he went on, 'but is there any chance that you could find it in you to fall in love with someone else?'

She was fighting a raging battle against the instinct that was in her to confess to him then and there that she *had* fallen in love, and that the man she had fallen in love with was him.

'Who—who did you have in mind?' she asked, picking her words as carefully as he had done.

'I wouldn't countenance you falling in love with anyone other than me,' Tallis told her, with a hint of his old aggression.

'Oh,' said Georgina, still not able to believe she was on very safe ground. 'Er—why should I want to do that?'

'God knows. I've given you very little cause to love me, the way I've behaved,' he said gruffly. 'But it's the only way I can think of to get this nightmare weight of jealousy off my shoulders and return me to being a right-minded normal-thinking, reasonable human being.'

'Oh,' said Georgina again, terrified of putting even the tiniest foot wrong. 'Are you—er—are you saying that—that you—er—l-love me?' As soon as she had said it, she wished she hadn't, and a fire of red burnt her skin.

'I've been telling you exactly that for the last ten minutes,' he said on a quiet growl, as though he had never told any woman before that he loved her, and found the telling difficult. Then, all man that he was, he rode on top of the unexpected reserve she was witnessing, and told her clearly, 'Georgina Underwood, I love you dearly, and I want you for my wife.'

'Oh,' said Georgina, then, 'Oh, Tallis!' then, her heart brimming, 'Oh, Tallis, I love you so very much, I've been making myself ill with it!'

Then as she watched and saw the great look of overwhelming joy that grew on his face, she knew she had been right to tell him. He looked stunned too, she thought, and it was instinct that had her leaning forward and placing her lips warmly against his.

And that was when Tallis took over. 'I warned you not to do that again unless you were ready to face the consequences,' he told her, his voice sounding as choked as hers had done. And then the magic of his kisses was hers as they both went out of control at the thought that all they wanted was theirs.

Tallis turned her on the settee, his lips covering her face with kisses, receiving a response from her that was as natural, free and uninhibited as the love she felt for him. 'My darling, darling,' Tallis whispered, his mouth just below her ear as he thrilled her with his ardency.

Held in his arms, Georgina thought herself in heaven. His hands caressed her and he poured out his love and need for her—told her of the pain loving her had caused him, and heard in return how she had come to love him, and her own pain in that loving.

'You'll never be hurt again, my darling, as long as I live,' he vowed, and then all was silent as his need for her and her need for him had them straining to each other.

It was only when she felt his hands warm on her skin that Georgina, lost in the wonder of finding herself loved, came out of her euphoric state, and the demon she wished buried nudged her, causing her to grow anxious lest Tallis in his discovery should laugh at her. Her arms slackened about him, and Tallis, his lips warm on the swell of her breasts, lifted his head, his eyes dark with desire.

'Something wrong, darling?' he asked gently, already, it seemed, tuned into her every change of wavelength.

'C-can we sit up for a while?' she asked hesitatingly, her face burning.

'You love me?' Tallis asked, puzzled.

'Oh yes, Tallis, yes, yes, yes!' Georgina replied urgently,

terrified he would go cold on her. But he managed to find a smile for her.

'You do pick your moments, my love,' he said softly. 'But as long as I know you love me—yes, we'll sit up.'

Georgina knew she was going to have to explain why she had called a halt to their lovemaking, but she just hadn't been able to go through with it, not for him to find out . . .

Had she imagined it would be any easier to tell him sitting up than lying down, she knew herself mistaken. For she was trembling with nerves, so that Tallis took one look at her, leaned forward and buttoned her shirt, then sat and put an arm around her.

'Something worrying you, Georgina?' he asked, and when she could only nod, he coaxed, 'Come on, my love. We love each other, what else matters?'

Stiltedly, she began, 'You know when—you know when we kissed before—well, then you thought I didn't want to because of—— Well, it had nothing to do with anyone else, but to do with me.'

'With you?' Tallis repeated, his tone unbearably understanding, she thought, just knowing that understanding was going to turn into highly amused laughter.

'Yes—well—oh, Tallis, I can't bear that you should laugh at me,' she blurted out.

'Laugh at you, darling?' he echoed, trying to hide his mystification by keeping his voice even. 'Why should I laugh at you?'

'Because,' she said, nearly going under with embarrassment, 'because had we—had I not—had we gone on, you would have found out . . .'

'Found out?' he prompted.

'I'm twenty-six,' she reminded him, her colour high. 'A girl about town, and with my own flat. I've never been hard up for dates when I wanted them. And . . . and I know this is supposed to be the permissive age and all that—but I've never ...' she gave an agonised moan as she came to the last bit, 'Oh, Tallis,' she said, 'I'm twenty-six and ... I'm still a—virgin.'

The minute the words were out she leaned forward and buried her head in his shoulder. If those shoulders began to shake then she would know he was laughing. She felt miserable after so much happiness, miserable, juvenile, and she could feel the tears coming to the surface.

But she found she had no need for those tears, for very gently, while still holding on to her, Tallis pushed her slowly back until he could see into her self-ashamed face. And when she did dare to look at him, she saw for herself that he wasn't laughing, but had such a look of adoration on his face, it was as though what she had just told him, instead of, as she had thought, making him laugh had touched him so much that he looked ready to worship her.

'You—didn't laugh,' she said hoarsely.

'My dearest, *dearest* Georgina,' he said, his voice thick in his throat, 'dearest girl, don't you know you are bringing me your most precious possession? Come here and let me kiss you.'

It was a kiss without passion, a kiss that told her how deeply Tallis loved her, for almost at once he pulled away from her.

'My beautiful, sensitive Georgina,' he said tenderly, 'I love you with all my heart. But in the light of what you've just told me, I think we'd better put your engagement ring on your finger and first thing in the morning set about seeing how quickly we can get its counterpart in place.'

Georgina was ecstatically happy. Tallis hadn't laughed at her. He loved her and wanted to marry her. The ring had fallen between the cushions and Tallis, still with that look of adoration in his eyes, placed it over her engagement finger.

'I think,' he said, his decision already made, 'we'd better telephone Maggie and warn your family that they'll be expected to attend a wedding in Kenilworth before the month is out. Do you agree?'

Georgina turned up her face to his, something inside her telling her Tallis might not be kissing her the way he had done until that wedding band was on her finger.

'The sooner the better,' she said, laughing up at him, and knew he had caught her meaning when he tipped back his head and roared.

'Hussy,' he grinned, and dropped a light kiss on the end of her nose before stretching out a hand to pass the telephone over to her. 'Dial,' he ordered.

Choose from this great selection of early
Harlequins—books that let you escape to
the wonderful world of romance!*

*Some of these book were originally published under different titles.

Relive a great love story...
Harlequin Romances 1980
Complete and mail this coupon today!

Harlequin Reader Service

In U.S.A.
MPO Box 707
Niagara Falls, N.Y. 14302

In Canada
649 Ontario St.
Stratford, Ontario, N5A 6W2

Please send me the following Harlequin Romance novels. I am enclosing my check or money order for $1.25 for each novel ordered, plus 59¢ to cover postage and handling.

☐ 422	☐ 509	☐ 636	☐ 729	☐ 810	☐ 902
☐ 434	☐ 517	☐ 673	☐ 737	☐ 815	☐ 903
☐ 459	☐ 535	☐ 683	☐ 746	☐ 838	☐ 909
☐ 481	☐ 559	☐ 684	☐ 748	☐ 872	☐ 920
☐ 492	☐ 583	☐ 713	☐ 798	☐ 878	☐ 927
☐ 508	☐ 634	☐ 714	☐ 799	☐ 888	☐ 941

Number of novels checked @ $1.25 each = $_____

N.Y. State residents add appropriate sales tax $_____

Postage and handling $_____ .59

TOTAL $_____

I enclose _____
(Please send check or money order. We cannot be responsible for cash sent through the mail.)

Prices subject to change without notice.

NAME _____
(Please Print)

ADDRESS _____

CITY _____

STATE/PROV. _____

ZIP/POSTAL CODE _____

Offer expires May 31, 1981

0115633